REPOSSESSION

(SAVAGE HELL MC BOOK 2)

K. L. RAMSEY

REPOssession

(Savage Hell MC Book 2)

BY K.L. Ramsey

REPOssession (Savage Hell MC Book 2)

Copyright © 2020 by K.L. Ramsey.

Cover design: Michelle Sewell- RLS Images Graphics and Designs

Imprint:Independently published

First Print Edition: July 2020

All rights reserved.

No part of this book may be reproduced, scanned, or distributed in any printed or electronic form without permission. Please do not participate in or encourage piracy of copyrighted materials in violation of the author's rights. Thank you for respecting the hard work of this author.

This is a work of fiction. Names, characters, places, and incidents either are the product of the author's imagination or are used fictitiously, and any resemblance to locales, events, business establishments, or actual persons— living or dead—is entirely coincidental.

CAT

Catrina Linz stood by the vending machine, handcuffs still on, waiting for her bail bondsman to show up. When she called the company she found in the ancient phone book, the guys baritone voice grumbled something about waking him up and getting him out of his warm bed. Cat wanted to point out that it was the middle of summer in Alabama and nearly a hundred degrees out. Everywhere was warm, so his argument didn't hold water, as her grandmother used to say. She just wanted to get home and wash away this whole fucking day and every one of the assholes who had used her body for their pleasure. Honestly, it had been a slow day. Fuck, if she was being completely honest, she'd admit that it had been a damn slow month. Cat wasn't sure how she was going to pay her rent and now, she was going to have to come up with the money to pay back her bail bondsman.

She slumped down into the chair next to the window. Maybe it was time to go back home and try to find some former semblance of her old life but that would mean she'd have to face her mother and her shitty step-father again. Hell, they'd probably insist that she admit she made the whole damn story up but, she hadn't. He was the no-good disgusting fucker she claimed he was. He raped her, taking her virginity when she was only fourteen and told her that if she told her mother, he'd kill her and her little brother. Cat kept her fucking mouth shut and what did her good old stepdad do? He rewarded her by repeatedly raping her for the next two years. That was when she told her mother—the one person on the planet who should have had her back. She was the one woman who should have believed her and protected her but she hadn't. Instead, her mother accused her of being a slut and seducing her step-father. Her mom kicked her out and stayed with that douche and Cat's only regret was having to leave her little brother, Liam, behind. He was four years younger than she was and she knew that dragging him with her would be no life for a kid. She was just a kid herself but the world had taught her the hard way that sometimes, the only thing you can do is run. So, that's what she did. Cat ran and when she got tired of running, she ran some more. There wasn't any amount of distance that she could put between her and her step-father that would make her feel safe. She'd never feel that way again—safe, wanted, loved. Not that it mattered. Cat wasn't sure she had ever experienced any of those feelings in her short life—

which sucked. Most women her age were married and had a kid or two. At twenty-seven, she decided that ship had left the harbor. Besides, who would want a woman as used up as she was?

"Cat Linz?" a very tall, tattooed guy looked her over and she squinted her eyes at him, trying to decide if she wanted to admit that he had the right person or send him packing. Honestly, the guy looked like one of her Johns and maybe he had been. With her luck, he was just some asshole who had paid her for sex. His smile was easy and God, he was good looking. Sure, it was in a surly hot biker kind of way, but if she had a type—this guy would fit it. That was one of the occupational hazards she faced though—every guy had to be her type or at least she had to pretend that was the case. His brown eyes were so dark, she was sure she could see her reflection in them and fuck, she looked like shit. He pushed his overly long brown hair back from his eyes and handed her a business card. She took it and tried to turn it over to read it, but that feat felt impossible, given her constraints.

"You wanna help me out, here?" she asked, shoving the card back in his direction. The guy had the nerve to laugh and he took the card from her and turned it over, putting it back between her hands.

"Sorry," he said. "I'm Repo."

Now it was her turn to giggle, "As in like—you're repossessing a car?" she teased.

He shrugged, "Sure," he agreed. "But I repossess people. I'm your bail bondsman. Well, that is if you're Catrina Linz."

"Yeah," she breathed. "That's me. How much is this going to set me back?" she asked.

"Not much into small talk? I like that. I'm not either. Fifteen hundred. I pay upfront and you pay me back. We can sign the papers when they process you for release. You don't pay me back on time—I find you. You run—"

"Let me guess, you find me?" she sassed. He rolled his eyes and nodded.

"This isn't something I take lightly. This is business," Repo spat.

"Fine," she said. "I agree. Just get me the fuck out of here." Repo called for one of the officers to help process her for release. This was only the third time she had been picked up for working the corner. How the hell was she supposed to know that the guy who picked her up tonight was a cop? Wasn't that entrapment or something? That was a question she'd ask her court-appointed lawyer because she certainly couldn't afford one. She just hoped that whoever got stuck with her case was willing to meet her on the street because that would be where she'd be living. Once she got back to her shithole apartment she was pretty sure her landlord would be waiting for his rent. When she'd finally get around to telling him she doesn't have it again this month, he was going to toss her out on her ass. He had been threatening to do it for weeks now and she was out of time and excuses.

"Can we hurry this up? I have an apartment to be kicked out of and a street bench to claim?" Repo chuckled as if she was kidding but none of this was a joke to her. The cop removed her cuffs and handed her a baggie full of her things.

Repo gave her the paperwork and a pen. "Read it over and if you have any questions, let me know." She smiled up at him and turned to the last page to fill out the personal information he required and signed her name on the line. She shoved the papers and pen back at him and he smiled at her. "Okay then," he said, taking the papers back from her. "Good doing business with you," he said. Cat watched as he turned the corner and then looked back.

"You were kidding about having to sleep on a bench, right? I mean, I'm only asking because I'll need an address to track you down in case you try to skip out on the cash I just put up for your ass." Repo didn't bother to walk back to where she was standing, just shouting his question for all the precinct to hear. Not that she cared. Cat stopped caring what other people thought about her a damn long time ago.

"I don't kid around a whole lot, Repo," she shouted back. "Business hasn't been that great and well, I don't have my rent. So yeah, I'm going to be evicted as soon as I get home. I'm betting my shit is already sitting by the curb, as we speak."

"Fuck," he cursed and walked back to her.

"I'm going to need an address or this won't work. You gave your friend Candy as your point of contact. Can you crash at her place?" She winced at his question. She sort of made that part up. She knew some woman named Candy but she had no idea where she lived. She was just some chick she sometimes passed the time with while they waited for their next clients. Candy was trying to get her to sign on with Sly—her pimp but that wasn't something Cat wanted. She had always gone it alone and if she couldn't make it in Huntsville, Alabama, she'd find another place to run to because that's what she was good at.

REPO

"Listen, how about we go out to the parking lot and you let me work off my debt with you and we can call it even?" The hot little piece of ass had landed herself in jail for prostitution and still hadn't learned her lesson.

"You must give a pretty spectacular blow job, Honey," he teased, "if you think you'll be able to work off the whole fifteen hundred." Cat smirked up at him and he knew she was going to give him some smart ass response. "You didn't learn anything from your few hours behind bars, did you, Honey?"

"I'm sorry, I didn't know that having a personal epiphany was part of the deal," she sassed. "So, how about it—you game?" she asked. God help him, Repo loved his women mouthy. It was usually the type of woman he picked up at the bar, Savage Hell, and took back to his place. He found that women who hung out at the MC were always looking to hook up with a biker in hopes of becoming his Ol'lady. Problem was—he had no plans of ever making any woman his for long term. He was more of a one night kind of guy. It worked for him but he was bright enough to know that if he took sexy little Cat up on her offer, he'd be out fifteen hundred and he needed that money back for his next bond.

He was always chasing the next job, hoping to find someone who fucked up big time and had no one else to call but him. He needed a big score if he planned on staying ahead of the rest of the games in town. Repo ran a respectable business and he wasn't going to run the risk of fucking that all up now over one willing woman.

"Not a chance, Honey," he breathed. "How about you just give me a real address that I'll be able to use to track you down and we can both get on with our days?" Cat had the nerve to lean into his body and pout. She smelled like sex and other men, a complete turn off for Repo. He didn't do sloppy seconds. Hell, he liked a woman who had been around and had some experience. He knew he could be a little rough with them and not worry about first times and all that bullshit. But, knowing that Cat had been on the job today, so to speak, was a complete turn off for him.

"Not going to happen, Cat," he growled.

"Well, I'm not sure what else I can offer you, Repo," she said. "I have no place to stay and in just a few hours, I'm pretty sure I'll be homeless. You have my cell, isn't that enough?" Repo ran his hand down his beard, trying to decide if he could trust Cat or not. His answer was a resounding, "Fuck no," but he had no other choice.

"Fine," he agreed. He pulled his cell from his jeans and dialed the number she had given him. Her cell phone chimed and she pulled it out of her purse.

"What are you doing?" she asked.

"I'm checking to make sure you didn't give me a bogus cell number," he admitted. She made a disgruntled noise in the back of her throat and he chuckled. "You really can't blame me, Cat. You haven't been on the up and up with me." She smiled and nodded.

"Got it," she grumbled. "You don't trust me—understood. Can I go now? I'd like to try to get a shower in before my landlord finds out that I'm home and tosses me out."

"Fine," he said. "But don't disappear Cat. You run and—" Cat held up her little hand, effectively stopping the rest of the words from coming out of his mouth.

"You'll find me," she finished for him. He watched her as she walked out of the station, sure that she was going to give him trouble. He could tell by the scared look in her eyes that she was going to run and God help him, he would do everything in his power to track her down. What he'd do with her next was up to her, but Repo had a feeling he would like his options.

CAT

Cat knew she was tempting fate but she had to go back to her shitty apartment to at least get her stuff. She was hoping to have a quick shower but when she showed up to her place and found a padlock on the front door and everything she owned piled into two cardboard boxes, she figured that was out of the question. Yeah, her landlord was fed up and sending her a message that she was receiving loud and clear. Her days of living in the luxury of her shitty, rathole, one-bedroom apartment were over and good riddance too.

"Shit," she grumbled. She picked up her two boxes of crap and started for the stairwell. She had just about made it down to the front of the damn building when her smarmy landlord stepped out in front of her. Cat didn't stop in time, instead running into a wall of overweight, stale beer smelling, cigarette smoking, disgusting, sweaty man.

"Pete," she spat, trying not to drop her two boxes.

"You were trying to sneak out of here without paying me your back rent, weren't you?" Pete asked. He looked her body over and she wanted to vomit. Cat could read every disgusting thought that had just run through her landlord's mind and God help her, she wouldn't be able to go through with whatever he was about to ask her to do.

"Not going to happen, Pete," she said.

"The way I see it is this, Cat," he started. "You either give me my money or I'll work it out of you. I'm sure we can think of a few ways for you to pay me back, Darlin'," he offered. Pete ran his dirty hand down her cheek and she could taste the stomach bile that rose to her mouth. Cat was good at focusing on anything other than her job while she was doing it but Pete made her physically ill.

She shrugged his hand off and he laughed. "I take it you have the cash then?" he asked. She didn't but telling him that wouldn't happen.

"Sure," she lied. "Could you hold my boxes for me so I can grab it?" Pete eyed her suspiciously and she thought the asshole was actually smart enough to see through her.

"All right," he said. "But if you try anything Cat, I'll fucking kill you and then do what I want with you."

"You're disgusting," she spat, thrusting her boxes at the fat bastard. "Hold these," Cat ordered. Pete reluctantly took her boxes and she saw her opportunity—her only way out and if it didn't work, she believed that Pete would carry through with his threat. He'd kill her and then violate her body and not think twice about what kind of human being that made him.

Cat decided to take her chance, hit her mark, and run like fuck to get away from him. She brought her knee up to meet the slime ball's nuts and when he doubled over in pain, she grabbed one of her boxes before it hit the ground and ran like hell. She didn't look back, leaving her other box and Pete both lying on the floor.

"You bitch," he shouted after her. "I'll find you and I'll kill you," he promised.

Cat ran for as long and far as she could and when she finally felt like she couldn't run anymore, she found an empty park bench and slumped onto it, trying to catch her breath.

"Fucking Pete," she breathed. Cat quickly looked around the empty park to make sure she wasn't followed—not that she expected Pete to be able to keep up with her. Even toting her box full of crap she was faster than the fat slob. She had ended up in the little park adjacent to the courthouse and she wanted to laugh at the irony. She had just left there and if she was a betting woman, she was pretty sure that after her arraignment she was going to end up back there—this time for an extended stay.

"Now what?" she whispered to herself. It had been a shit day. Hell, if she was being honest, it had been a shit few years but surviving was proving to be more difficult than she planned when she left home. A part of Cat wondered if she wouldn't have been better off staying at home and letting her step-father have his way with her. At least she'd be off the street and sleeping in a warm bed every night. Instead, she was hungry, cold, and used up. Cat wasn't sure what her next step should be but at twenty-seven, she was about ready to throw in the damn towel. Giving up would be easier than any of this shit but that wasn't who she was. Cat prided herself for being strong and able to survive just about any shit life wanted to throw at her but she wasn't sure if she'd be able to get through this. She was homeless and helpless with no real ideas of what the fuck to do next.

Cat curled up into a ball on the hard metal bench, pulling her knees to her chest. She allowed herself to cry because she had earned it. It felt like the only thing left to do. After all, she was only human and had reached the end of her rope. She cried because it was all she had left.

REPO

Repo was called back down to the courthouse by the same officer who arrested Catrina Linz earlier that day. The officer's shift was ending and he had found Cat sleeping on a park bench across the street from the courthouse. The guy was nice enough to say that he didn't want Repo to lose his bail bond when she ran. He thanked the guy and jumped back into his pick-up truck to head over to the little park. He needed to figure out what the hell he was going to do with Cat because the last thing he wanted to do was lose another bail bond. If Cat ran, she'd be the third to take off on him that month and at that rate, he'd be out of money and out of business in no time.

All Repo wanted to do was get on his bike and ride over to his club, Savage Hell, drink the night away and find a biker fly to spend his night with. But, with each passing hour, he was beginning to realize that wasn't going to happen tonight. Still, he needed to call Savage to let him know that he wasn't going to make it to church tonight which was a shame since they had some new probates coming in and he always loved to give them some shit.

Savage answered on the first ring, "Lo," he said.

"Hey man," Repo said. Savage grunted into the other end of the cell and Repo knew he was catching his club's Prez at a bad time. "Shit, sorry," Repo said. He heard some rustling on the other end of the line and Dallas' giggle. Yeah, he had interrupted something, if he was guessing correctly, Savage wasn't going to be very happy with his intrusion. "Tell Bowie and Dallas I'm sorry," Repo offered.

"What can I do for you, Repo?" Savage asked, sighing into the phone.

"Nothing really," Repo said. "I just wanted to let you know that it looks like I'll be working tonight and won't be able to make it to church. Can you manage without me?" As one of the older members, Savage counted on him to keep the guys patching into Savage Hell in check. The younger guys like to bend the rules sometimes to see how much Savage and the rest of the club would be willing to let them get away with. Savage would lose his fucking mind if it wasn't for some of the other guys, like Repo, stepping up as enforcers to keep the probies in line.

"We'll manage," Savage said. "You do what you have to and stay safe out there, man."

"Will do," Repo agreed. "I'll be in tomorrow night if all

goes as planned. I'm not sure how much trouble this case is going to give me but if she runs, I'm out money and I can't let that happen."

"Understood," Savage said. "See you on the flip side." Savage ended the call and Repo tossed his cell on the seat next to him. He pulled into the parking lot across from the courthouse and spotted Cat as soon as he got out of his truck. Sure enough, the cop had given him good intel—she was asleep on one of the benches, clutching a cardboard box to her chest. If he was guessing correctly that box looked to contain all her worldly possessions and God if that didn't tug at his fucking heart.

Cat Linz seemed to be doing a lot of that today—making him feel things he usually didn't. Things like pity and compassion and hell, maybe even a little lust. "Hey," he shouted, carefully poking her sleeping form with his boot-clad foot. "Wake up, Cat," he ordered. She stirred and moaned, trying to roll over to get comfortable on the hard bench again only to flip onto the ground. She sat up and looked around as if trying to figure out how she ended up there. Cat looked up at Repo and squinted her eyes at him.

"You," she spat. "You pushed me onto the ground," she accused.

"No," he said. "You did that all by yourself. I was just trying to wake your ass up. Why the fuck are you sleeping on a park bench across the street from the courthouse?" Repo questioned.

Cat stood up and brushed herself off, picking up her box

and belongings, tossing them onto the bench. "Well, the Ritz has no vacancies, so here I am." She held her arms wide and spun around slowly giving Repo a good look at her curvy, sexy body. Yeah, she was fucking hot but Repo needed to remember that Cat Linz was a job—a paycheck and he never fucked with his money.

"Yeah," she breathed. "Take a good look, fucker. The first look's free but the next one will cost you," Cat sassed.

"Thanks, Honey. I'm good with just one look though," Repo taunted. Cat dropped her arms to her sides and blew out her breath. "How about you tell me what you're really doing here on this bench?"

"I already told you earlier," she spat, "I was evicted. My landlord has this crazy thing where he likes to get paid his rent to let me live in my apartment."

"Yeah," Repo said. "I hear that's the way things are usually done. I take it you didn't have the money to pay him then?"

Cat slumped to the bench and shrugged. "Things have been slow lately."

"Ah, a decline in business or unhappy customers?" Repo teased. He knew he was egging her on and probably going to catch hell from her for doing it but he didn't give a fuck—she was fun to spar with.

Cat stood and put both hands on her hips, "I do not have unhappy customers," she insisted. "I don't have a pimp, so having to go this alone makes things a little harder. Other girls have no problem getting called but I don't have someone helping to find—um well, work," she squeaked. "So, yeah—things are tight right now and my scumbag landlord kicked me out."

"What about all your stuff?" Repo asked, eyeing the lone cardboard box sitting next to her on the park bench.

Cat looked down at her box and back up at him. "This is about it," she whispered. "I had one other box but had to leave it behind."

"Too heavy?" Repo asked. He hated that he cared. He hated that she was sucking him into her story and her life. This wasn't who he was. Repo wasn't the type of guy who gave a fuck about anyone's sad story. He learned at a young age that helping others usually cost him something so he usually steered clear of getting involved in other people's messy lives. It just made things easier that way.

"No," Cat said. "I couldn't go back for it without giving that slimeball a chance to get his hands on me."

"Your landlord?" Repo asked, trying to keep up.

"Yeah," she said. "Let's just say he had a few ideas of how I could work off my back rent with him and I wasn't willing to suck his dirty cock." Cat stared Repo down as if daring him to say something.

He held up his hands, as if in defense. "I'm not judging you, Cat. That's not what's happening here."

"All right," she said. "Then why are you here, Repo, was it?" she asked. She knew damn good and well what his name was.

Repo smirked and nodded. "Yeah," he said. "But, you

already knew that. As for why I'm here, Cat, I told you that if you run—I'll find you."

"Technically, I haven't run. Well, unless you count running from my asshole landlord to get here. I'm not going anywhere, Repo. I can't afford to—so, if you need me, I will be right here." She sat down on the bench again and patted the metal seat. "We good here?"

"Hardly," he said. "I can't leave your ass sitting here on this fucking bench, Cat."

She smirked up at him, "Aw, a bond bailsmen with a heart of gold—that it, Repo?"

"You really are a pushy little bitch, aren't you Cat? No, I've never been accused of having a heart of gold," Repo insisted. "In fact, I've been told that I'm a heartless bastard by quite a few of my friends."

"Well, with friends like that—" she stared.

"We aren't friends either," Repo said, pointing between Cat and himself. "This is business," he said.

"I get it, Repo—you're not here out of the goodness of your heart. Understood but the fact remains that I have no place to go but this bench here. You seem to want that not to be true, Repo but here I am—homeless and bench bound. As soon as I can find some work, I'll try to get some cash together to find a cheap place to crash. But for now, I'm home," she said. Repo cringed when she mentioned finding work. He knew what that would entail and although he wasn't a prude, Cat working could land her back behind bars again and his chances of getting his money back would go down the toilet with her freedom.

"You a first-time offender?" he asked. She looked at him like he lost his mind.

"Sorry," she said.

"Have you ever been arrested and tried for prostitution before today?" he clarified.

"I've been picked up two other times but the officer who brought me in was very—accommodating, let's just say." Repo knew that there were a lot of corrupt cops in the system who'd be all too willing to let sexy little Cat give him a blow job for her "Get out of jail free card".

"So, this will be the first time you'll be arraigned?" Repo asked. Cat nodded and he was pretty sure that what he was going to say next would qualify him as a complete fucking lunatic. "Fine, you're coming home with me until we can work this all out."

"That's a really bad fucking idea," Cat said. She looked him up and down again like he was out of his mind and yeah, he was. But, he had made the offer and he wouldn't take it back now.

"Listen," he barked. "I don't like this any more than you do but I need to keep an eye on you and make sure you show up for court. Your case should be on the docket in a couple of weeks and well, I think I can go that long without strangling you," he joked.

"Yeah well, I don't know if I can make you the same promise, big guy," Cat grumbled.

Repo barked out his laugh. "I'm not too worried about that. And, I'm not asking you if you want to come home with me. I'm telling you to get your fucking box and get in my truck. I've already lost a few other bails with runners this month. I don't have the money, time or energy to track you down if you take off and Cat—you look like a runner. So, get your shit and get your ass in my truck."

Cat stood and he could see the fight in her eyes and that was the last thing he needed right now. He sighed, knowing that she was going to make him do this the hard way. "Suit yourself," he growled. Repo picked Cat up and flung her over his shoulder like she weighed close to nothing. He picked up her box and when she started to give him some fight, he swatted her ass.

"Stay the fuck still or I'll taser you and then throw your body into the bed of my pick-up. I'm done fucking around with you, Cat," Repo said.

"You can't force me to do this, Repo," she shouted. "You're kidnapping me—taking me against my will. I don't want this and I don't want you," she spat.

"Feelings mutual, Honey. I don't fucking want you either but I don't give a fuck what you want. As soon as your court case is over, you'll be free to go on your way. Until that happens, you will follow my rules to a tee," Repo said.

"Or what?" Cat asked.

"Or I'll lock you in your fucking room and you'll live like my fucking prisoner instead of my guest. Your call, Cat," he said. Repo knew he wasn't playing nicely but he just didn't care. His unwanted house guest was going to learn quickly just who was in charge. She seemed to lose some of her fight and he unlocked his truck, practically tossing both her and her box into the passenger seat.

"And, Cat—you try to run and," he started but he should have known she'd want the last word.

"And, you'll find me," she spat.

He smiled and nodded, "See, now you're catching on," Repo taunted, slamming her door shut.

CAT

REPO DROVE IN SILENCE AND THAT WAS FINE BY HER. A PART OF her wondered where he was taking her but for the most part, she didn't give a fuck. She had already fallen so low that getting out of the pit she was in felt damn near impossible. Repo turned into an apartment complex and parked his truck, cutting the engine.

"This is me," he almost whispered.

"So, you weren't kidding when you said that you were going to take me back to your place," Cat said.

"I don't kid—ever," Repo said. "I told you back at the park that I plan on keeping a close eye on you, Cat."

She looked him over and smiled, "How close are we talking?" Cat asked.

Repo shook his head, "Not that close," he protested. "I don't fuck with my work and Cat—you're my work."

"So, no sex then?" she asked. Honestly, a part of her was feeling a little let down by his denial. It would be so much easier to persuade Repo to just let her go if he'd agree to have sex with her. Using her body to get what she wanted had become second nature to her.

"No," he breathed. "At least, not between the two of us. I think we need to set a few ground rules before you get the wrong idea of what's going to happen here," Repo said.

"I'm really tired and need a shower," she said, scrunching up her nose. Cat knew she must stink and honestly, a hot shower sounded like heaven. "Can talking wait until later?" Or Never. Cat was pretty sure she wasn't going to get that lucky though judging by the determination she saw on Repo's handsome face. He stroked his beard as if he was thinking about it but she already knew what his answer was going to be. There was no way he'd let her off that easy.

"No," he said again.

"I'm beginning to wonder if you don't have many words to draw from in your vocabulary, Repo," Cat teased. "You seem to be saying no an awful lot."

"You aren't giving me much cause to use my words, Cat. I'll show you my spare bedroom and make us sandwiches while you take your shower. But then, you and I are going to have a come to Jesus meeting and I won't take no for an answer," he insisted.

"Fine," she spat. "But, you can't keep me here against my will. That's called kidnapping," she said. Repo got out of his truck and she jumped down out of the passenger's side of his pick-up and grabbed her box from the seat, following him up to his second-floor apartment. Repo moved fast and Cat was so tired she was having trouble keeping up with him.

"You're right, I can't keep you here without your consent," he said back over his shoulder as he unlocked his front door. "What I can do is call the sheriff's office and tell them that you are a flight risk and have you arrested. Hell, I'll drag your ass down to the station myself and watch as they slap the cuffs on you," Repo said.

Cat followed him into his apartment and looked around. She had never been in a place so nice. Sure, a few of her clients had her meet them at nice hotels but most guys had her suck them off in the front seat of their cars or some sleazy ass motel. It was easier that way since most of them had wives and families. The men she met usually had limited funds and time—which was fine by her. As long as they had the money to pay her, she didn't care how much time they spent with her. In fact—the less time she had to spend with her clients, the better.

Repo walked down the small hallway, flicking on lights as he went and stood outside of one of the bedrooms. "This is you," he said. "I'm sure you saw the kitchen and living room on our way back here. It's not a very big place but it's home for now."

Cat nodded, "Sure," she said. "It's the nicest place I've ever stayed," she admitted. She sounded just as pathetic as her statement made her feel but she never really gave a fuck about what anyone thought of her. She wasn't going to start now no matter how Repo looked at her like he pitied her.

"Your apartment was bad, huh?" Repo asked. Bad was an understatement. Her building should have been condemned and her landlord made slum lords look like decent human beings.

"You could say that," she said.

"Well, feel free to help yourself to just about anything in the apartment but stay the fuck out of my room," he said, nodding to the end of the hallway.

"I assume that's your room?" Cat taunted, pointing to the closed door.

"Yeah," he said. "You have a bathroom attached to your bedroom, so we won't have to share. I figure that's for the best—you know, giving us both privacy so we don't walk in on the other."

"God forbid," she teased. Cat walked into her room and dropped her box on the bed. "Um—" she squeaked. "I don't have a change of clothes. The other box—the one I had to leave behind, had all my clothing in it. Do you have a t-shirt I could borrow for the night?"

"Yeah—wait here," Repo ordered. He disappeared down the hall into his bedroom, shutting the door behind himself after he went in. He returned to her room and handed her a few neatly folded t-shirts.

"You can borrow these and I'll see what I can do to rustle you up a few things. You look to be about the same size as some of my club's Ol'ladies," Repo said.

"Who?" Cat asked.

"It's an MC thing. I'm in a club and that's what we call our women. Anyway, I know that a few of the women wouldn't mind lending you a few things," Repo said. He turned to leave the room and Cat stood to find the bathroom, eagerly looking forward to a hot shower. "Meet me in the kitchen when you're done. Everything you need should be in the bathroom. I keep it pretty well stocked," he said over his shoulder.

"Thank you," she called after him as he disappeared down the hall. Repo hummed his reply and Cat shut the bedroom door and locked it out of habit. It was something she learned to do as a young girl, trying to make sure that she could take her showers in peace. Her step-father used to enjoy walking in on her under the pretense of not hearing the shower and when she asked him to leave, he'd usually laugh at her. She had no privacy unless her mother was home and locking the door was sometimes her only reprieve.

Cat quickly showered and slipped on Repo's t-shirt. It said, "Savage Hell" across the back and had skulls in what looked like a decal on the front. She smoothed it over her curves and looked at her reflection in the full-length mirror on the back of the bathroom door.

"Time to face the giant, angry man," she whispered to her reflection. Cat left the bedroom to pad down the hallway to find Repo. He was in the kitchen, as promised, making them sandwiches.

Repo looked her up and down and then nodded. "Hope

you're okay with grilled cheese," he said. "It's all I know how to make."

"I love grilled cheese," she said. "I'm starving, so anything works," she admitted. She was hungry too. The last time she ate was yesterday morning and living off coffee wasn't her best idea but she got it for free from the local gas station because she knew the manager. Hell, he was one of her customers and he told her to take some food too but she knew that she'd end up paying "extra" for his generosity, so she passed up his offer.

Repo nodded, handing her a plate with two sandwiches on it. "Did you have a nice shower?" he asked. Cat knew he was trying to make small talk and honestly, it was adorable but she wasn't a small talk kind of girl.

"Why am I here, Repo?" she asked, taking a bite of her sandwich. It tasted so good, she practically forgot to breathe while she inhaled the first half.

"Slow down, Cat," Repo said around a chuckle. "At the rate, you're going, you'll choke to death before you can grill me for more details. I told you earlier—you're here so I can keep an eye on you." Repo finished off his sandwich in just two big bites and Cat wanted to laugh at how much of a hypocrite he was about her eating her food too quickly.

"And, I've already told you that I don't need a babysitter, Repo," she said around a mouthful of sandwich. "I can manage on my own, just fine," she insisted.

"Sure," he said, grabbing another sandwich from the pan.

"You seemed to be doing great, sleeping on a park bench clutching a box with all your worldly belongings."

"I told you that I was evicted and the box didn't contain everything I own," she countered. Repo practically stood toe to toe with her and she could feel the heat rolling from his big body. He seemed to be turned on by their little give and take and if she was being honest, she was too.

"You like a woman who gives you a little hell, don't you, Repo?" she asked.

"Don't," he barked.

"Don't what?" she asked, taking a chance and stepping closer into his big body. Repo huffed out his breath and put his plate on the kitchen counter. He stared down at her as if daring her to make another move and she couldn't help her giggle. Sure, he was big and scary. Most women and men, for that matter, would find Repo standing over them imposing but Cat was never one to back down from a challenge.

"Don't push me, Cat. I told you that I don't fuck with my work and you're work right now." He stepped back from her and Cat wasn't sure if she felt more disappointed or relieved that he did. He was right, them getting involved would be a fucking mistake but he was fun to toy with and she was betting he'd be a lot of fun in bed too. But, that wouldn't happen because men like Repo didn't want a used up woman like her. She was sure that he didn't have any issues getting most of the female population to notice him with his muscles and tattoos in all the right places. He was big and had a bad boy image that most women would drop their panties for. She used to be one of those women but not anymore. Now, she was a prostitute, a call girl, a plaything for hire and that worked for her. It paid her bills most of the time and until recently, kept food in her belly and a roof over her head. Now that was all over for her unless she took Candy's pimp up on his offer.

Sly Blankenship looked harmless to most people. Hell, he looked like the all American boy next door and she was pretty sure that his rap sheet was squeaky clean too. Sly knew how to keep his nose out of trouble because when push came to shove, he'd let his girls take the rap for him. Candy had been picked up more times than Cat could keep track of, for working the same street corner as her. Every time her friend reappeared to work, she praised Sly for bailing her out but Cat knew that a good pimp would have made sure that Candy was working a corner that wasn't under surveillance. Hell, a good pimp wouldn't make his girls work a corner at all. It was old school and outdated, having to stand on a street corner and wait for an offer. No, Cat longed for classier calls where she'd meet her clients in their homes or hotel rooms. Occasionally, she got a few of those calls and God, the pay was great but here lately, the street corner was her only option.

And, good old Sly didn't like her working Candy's corner. If she was a gambler, she'd bet that Sly was the one who called her into the cops. She wouldn't put it past him to have set up the cop to make her an offer, landing her behind bars.

But, that was something she'd share with her court-appointed lawyer if she was ever assigned one.

"Hey," Repo said. "You okay?"

Cat nodded. "Yeah, sorry. I guess I've got a lot on my mind—it's been a damn long day. You mind if I hit the sheets?" she asked.

"No," Repo said. "I'm beat myself. I'll clean up here and then probably turn in too." Cat nodded and brushed past him to put her plate in the sink.

"Thanks for dinner, Repo. And, for the place to stay," she whispered. "I'll try to be out of your hair before you know it." She walked back to the spare bedroom and shut the door, locking it behind her. Yeah, just like the good old days.

REPO

Repo watched as Cat disappeared back to his spare room. He had just about swallowed his damn tongue when she appeared in his kitchen wearing the t-shirt he lent her and nothing else. God, she was gorgeous but he needed to keep his damn head on straight and remember that she was his job and once this mess was all over, she'd go back to the streets—back to the faceless, nameless men who paid her for sex. He didn't give a fuck where she had been but he wouldn't make her his knowing that it wouldn't change anything. She'd let other men have her body for money and that wasn't something he could live with.

He also knew that if given the chance, Cat would take off, leaving him high and dry. She wanted to run—he could see that in her eyes every damn time she looked at him. He knew all the signs because he used to be just like her. Repo's past was just as dark and seedy as he was betting Cat's was. That was something he could also see when she looked at him— the fear and self-loathing and yeah, he knew both well.

Repo lived on the streets for years after his mother died and his old man took off. It was either that or be tossed into the welfare system and hope like hell that he got in with a good family. He knew the odds of that happening were slim to none. Not many families wanted a sixteen-year-old teenager. There wasn't anything cute about a kid who looked like a full-grown man complete with facial hair and two tattoos. Yeah, he was past the whole, "I'm adorable, please adopt me," phase. He knew he needed to lay low and keep to himself for two years until he aged out of the system. No one was looking for him and no one cared whether he lived or died. Repo knew he had to count on himself and leave his past behind, so he changed his name from Tyler Morris to Repo and he assumed the badass persona that everyone knew him for.

Things were tough those two years and he had to do whatever it took to stay alive, including pimping himself out to whoever was paying—women and men alike, it didn't matter to him as long as they had cash. After he turned eighteen and he could come out of living in the shadows, he got a real job at a bike shop. It's where he discovered his love of motorcycles and he was able to leave his life of pimping himself out behind. He learned the ins and outs of the different bikes the little shop had and even figured out how to fix them. He made enough at his new job to get himself an apartment and save a little money to start up his bail bondsman business. He loved what he did for work and he made a good deal of money at his job. He was able to buy his cabin in Gatlinburg, Tennessee that he considered as close to heaven as he'd ever get.

Someday, Repo hoped to move back to Gatlinburg full time but right now, his place was in Huntsville, Alabama. It's where his life was—his club, his friends, and the majority of his business. When he first bought the cabin, he dreamed of meeting someone and settling down to start a family there. But after ten years, that was starting to feel more like a pipe dream and less like a possible reality. Still, he got home to his cabin as often as possible and what little time he spent there was pure heaven.

Repo got the kitchen cleaned up and settled on his sofa, pulling the blanket he kept thrown over the back of the couch onto his body. He didn't trust Cat as far as he could throw her and if his hunch was right, she was going to make a run for it. There was no way he'd miss her sneaking out of his apartment if he was asleep on his sofa. His living room was right off the entrance and if Cat tried to get out of his front door, he'd hear her. There was no way he'd let her just walk out of his apartment and out of his life.

Repo heard Cat trying to sneak past him, if that's what she was doing could be called. Honestly, she made more noise than an elephant trying to walk through an antique store. He laid as quiet as he could until she slipped on her shoes but that was as far as he let her get. If she walked out his door, he might never find her again and then he'd be out his bond money and that wasn't going to happen—not on his watch.

"Going someplace, Honey?" he asked.

Cat jumped and squealed, "Shit, Repo," she said. "You scared the fuck out of me."

Repo sat up on his sofa and turned on the overhead light. They both blinked against the brightness and when he got a good look at her Repo realized that she was wearing a black tank top and skintight jeans.

"Nice outfit," he taunted. "I thought you didn't have anything to wear?" he asked.

"I don't," Cat said. "Just this and my outfit you found me in and well, that was dirty." Repo had a pretty good idea why she needed a fresh outfit to go out but he didn't want to be right.

"Where you headed?" he questioned, already knowing the answer.

"I have a job," she almost whispered. "It's the only way I'll be able to get back on my feet and out of your hair."

"No," Repo spat. He stood from the sofa, letting his blanket fall to the floor. Cat looked him up and down, her eyes resting on his boxer briefs and he grabbed a throw pillow from his couch to cover up. "Jesus, Cat," he grumbled. "Stop looking at me like that," he ordered.

"Maybe put on some pants," she offered. "Listen, my client isn't going to wait outside for long," she said.

"Wait—you fucking gave your client my address and had him meet you here?" he asked. The last thing he needed was for anyone to think he was pimping out Cat and her clients, as she liked to call them, showing up at his home wasn't acceptable.

Cat shrugged and defiantly raised her chin. "Well, I'm not sure where we are or where the closest bus stop is. We both know I can't afford an Uber, so unless you have a better plan, I need to head out." He had a better plan—he had a fucking fantastic plan. He would just lock her in his spare room until her arraignment and then he'd drag her ass down to the courthouse himself. But she was right, he couldn't hold her prisoner no matter how much easier that sounded than having to deal with the shit she was giving him.

"You are not going out to work, Cat. I told you that you are staying here until your day in court. Once that happens, you are free to do as you please," he said.

Cat barked out her laugh, "Or, I'll be in prison for the next year and won't have a chance to get back on my feet once I get out. You know that when they finally release me, I'll be in this very same position, right? The only way I can plan is to make some money now and sock it away someplace safe for when I get out."

"Why do you think they'll put you away for a year?" he asked. He wasn't a lawyer but he had been around enough criminals to know some of the finer points of the law. She was a first-time offender and if he had to guess, she wasn't someone they'd want to make an example of. She didn't seem to be hooked on anything and she wasn't a threat to society. She was just a woman down on her luck and most of the time, the court would take pity on someone like her.

"You'll probably just get some community service and maybe have to pay a fine or time served with probation," he offered.

"And, your law degree is from where, exactly?" she asked, crossing her arms over her ample chest. Her tank top accentuated her every curve, making him want to throw his rule of not fucking with his money, out the window.

"I've been around enough to know how things run, Cat," Repo said. "You told me that this is your first court appearance." Cat nodded and looked down at her feet. The last thing he was trying to do was make her feel bad about who she was but that was all he seemed capable of doing around her.

"Yeah, the other two times, I was let go with a warning," she said.

"Sure," Repo said. "After you gave the cop a blow job, right?"

"Well, yeah. Figures you'd remember that part of the story. The point is, this is my first offense, as you already said. Do you think I'll get off easy?" she asked. Cat's phone chimed and she looked at it and back at him. He knew that she was trying to figure out her next move but what Cat didn't understand was that she wouldn't be leaving his apartment tonight with the guy who was waiting downstairs for her or anyone else for that matter.

"You want to let your client know that you won't be joining him or should I just run downstairs and tell him to fuck off?" he asked.

"You wouldn't," she breathed. "I told you I need the work, Repo."

"No, you don't. I told you that I'm not letting you out of my sight, Cat," he said. "The way I see it, you have two choices here. One—you text your waiting client and tell him to get lost."

"And, two?" she asked.

"Two—I'll go down and do it for you but I'll also make sure he gets arrested to boot. Your choice, Honey," he said.

"You're an asshole," Cat spat.

"Yeah, I've been told," Repo said. That wasn't the first time someone had called him that. Hell, he had been called worse most of his life. "What's it going to be, Cat?" Repo asked. He waited her out and could see the indecision on her face as she stared him down.

"Shit," she grumbled. "Fine." Cat pulled her phone back out of her back pocket and texted her waiting client. "There," she said. "Happy now?"

He wasn't happy about any of this. Hell, the only way he'd be happy was if he was asleep in his damn bed, preferably with a warm, willing woman—or two by his side. Repo walked over to the window and pulled the blinds to the side to watch for any movement in the parking lot. He spotted her client as he started his car and took off like a bat out of hell. Now, he was happy but he wasn't about to admit that to Cat.

"I'd love to get some shut-eye," he said. "You think you can behave yourself until morning?" Cat smirked and nodded, giving him his answer.

"Sure," she said.

"Now see, you're telling me, yes but I can tell by your expression that it's just not going to happen. Give me your phone," he insisted.

"My phone?" she gasped. "No fucking way," she hissed.

"Give me your fucking phone and then get your ass back to your bedroom, Cat. I'm done screwing around here. One thing you'll learn about me is if I'm tired, I'm not to be fucked around with. Phone," he shouted, holding out his hand waiting for her to comply. He wasn't sure what his next move would be if she refused but he was hoping he wouldn't have to worry about that. He stood there waiting and when a few minutes had passed, he almost gave up. Cat sighed and slapped the phone into the palm of his hand.

"Fine," she spat. "I'm going to sleep now, as long as that's all right with you, your worship," she sassed. Repo gave a mock bow and waved her past his body. She brushed passed him and he got a whiff of the strawberry-scented shampoo he kept in the spare bathroom. God, she smelled like heaven. Repo shook off her scent, trying to clear his head from the lust-filled haze. Not going to happen.

CAT

Cat tossed and turned for about an hour and then finally relaxed enough to fall asleep. When she woke up, she found a big, very pissed off Repo standing over her. "What the fuck," she gasped, scrabbling to make sure that her naked body was covered by the blankets. "I locked the fucking door, Repo," she spat. "How did you get in here?"

"It's my fucking apartment, Cat. Do you think I wouldn't be able to break into my damn spare room?"

Cat practically pulled her covers to her chin. "I'm naked under here, Repo," she said. He looked her over as if he could see straight through the thin barrier of blankets and sheets that covered her body. "I thought you said you don't fuck with your money," she whispered. Repo shook his head as if trying to erase the mental images he had conjured of her and nodded.

"Right," he agreed. "You want to tell me why you locked the fucking door, Cat?"

"Well, Dad," she teased, rolling her eyes.

"I'm not your father, Cat. If I was, you'd be over my knee and I'd be spanking your ass red by this point." Now it was her turn to feel a little hot and bothered. She looked Repo's body over, noticing that he was fresh from the shower and wearing just a pair of gym shorts and a t-shirt that hugged his muscles and showed off his impressive tattoos. Cat wondered if his entire torso was covered in ink and the thought of seeing him naked made her mouth water. It had been some time since she was turned on by just looking at a man. She had become so desensitized by sex and men that nothing seemed to turn her on anymore. The men she met up with for sex were just a job to her and nothing about pleasuring them was a turn on for her. Repo seemed to make her girly parts stand up and take notice which was a nice surprise.

"Spank me?" she questioned as if she didn't hear him quite right. She had never been spanked before and the thought of him doing that to her made her wet. Some of her clients liked things a little rough but she never let it get out of hand. Spanking, hitting, biting—they were all against the rules while she was working. But, she'd be willing to push her limits with Repo, if he was asking.

"No," he breathed. "Okay, that was a bad choice of words on my part. That's not going to happen between us, Cat, so wipe that thought right out of your head."

Cat gave a curt nod, "Right—no spanking then," she said feeling a little disappointed.

"You still haven't answered my question, Cat. Why did you lock yourself in here? Do I scare you?" Repo asked.

Repo was a big guy and he probably scared most people. His appearance was intimidating with his tattoos and bad boy biker vibes he was throwing out but he didn't scare her—not at all.

"No," Cat admitted. "I guess I locked it out of habit." She decided to give him a little part of the truth because the whole bit would make her sound pathetic.

"Habit," he repeated. "I get that you lived in a bad neighborhood but why would you lock your bedroom door?" he pushed. God, she hated that he wouldn't drop the whole subject. The last thing Cat wanted to do was spill her guts about her shitty upbringing. But, Repo was like a dog with a bone and she was sure he wouldn't let her slide with her partial truths.

"Fine," she spat. "I lock my bedroom door because it's what I had to do when I was a kid. My step-father figured out how to get past the locked door too—like you Repo." He took a step back from her, acting as if she had offended him in some matter.

"I—I wouldn't do that to you, Cat," he defended. "God, that happened to you?" he asked.

Cat nodded, "Yeah," she breathed. "I didn't mean to imply that you are anything like my asshole step-father."

"How old were you when it started?" Repo asked.

"Fourteen," she murmured. "It started when I was fourteen and went on for two years until I ran away." Repo crossed the small bedroom and sat on the edge of her bed.

"Shit, Cat," he grumbled. "Did you tell anyone?"

Cat barked out her laugh, "Not at first," she admitted. "I know how pathetic that makes me sound but when he told me that he'd kill my little brother, Liam if I told my mom, I believed him. When I turned sixteen, something inside of me switched on and I realized that the power he held over me was something I was allowing. I gave him my power by keeping my mouth shut. I finally broke down and told my mother."

"Wow," Repo breathed. "Good for you. What did she do? Is your step-father still in prison?" Cat's laughter rang through the room and Repo looked at her as if she lost her mind.

"He never went to prison. Hell, that fucker wasn't even arrested. My mother didn't believe me," she said. "She took his side in the whole thing—even going as far as to call me a slut and saying that I seduced him. What fourteen-year-old girl wants to lose her virginity to her step-father?" she questioned. Repo reached out and took her hand into his and Cat found the gesture to be so damn sweet, she couldn't help her tears. She wasn't a crier—never had been but it was like a dam broke inside of her and she couldn't hold them at bay one minute longer.

"Damnit," she cursed. "I never cry."

"It's all right, Cat. You don't have to be kick-ass tough all the damn time. You're a human being and allowed to break down once in a while," Repo insisted.

"I just don't want to give him my tears, you know? I've already given him so much of myself," she sobbed.

"Cat," Repo whispered. He scooted closer to her, pulling her into his arms and she willingly let him, taking the comfort he was offering. It had been so long since someone touched her like he was—just giving her comfort and not wanting anything in return from her. It felt good to have someone just want to hug her and not want a blow job for their efforts. Cat had forgotten what it felt like to have someone care about her or in this case—pretend to care. She sobbed into his t-shirt knowing that trying to hold back her tears was pointless. He was right, she could let herself grieve just this once, and then she'd push all the sadness and emotions back down where they belonged—below the surface. What had happened to her was dark and disgusting and should never see the light of day. Her past was too ugly—she was ugly and her step-father had made her that way.

"I'm so sorry, Honey," he whispered. "Your mother should have had your back—you were just a kid."

"Yeah well, she didn't," Cat said into his chest. "Instead, she kicked me out and that was fine by me since I was leaving anyway. There was no way I wanted to stick around and let that asshole continue to rape me. But, I had to leave Liam, my little brother. He was still a kid and I never knew if he made it out of that hellhole like I did." Leaving Liam was the only thing she regretted about leaving her childhood home. He was only twelve when she left.

"How old would your brother be now?" Repo asked, as if able to read her mind.

"About twenty-three," she said. "I tried to reach out to him a few times since he turned eighteen but he never responded." She shrugged like it wasn't a big deal but it was. "He probably bought into my mother and step-father's lies about me. I can't blame him. I just left him behind and he has to hate me for that."

Repo sweetly kissed the top of her head. "I seriously doubt your brother hates you, Honey. You were only doing what you had to. You got out of a horrible situation and found your way, doing the best you could in life."

Cat laughed, "Sure, a prostitute is the best I could do—thanks for that, Repo," she teased, trying to lighten the mood.

"That's not what I mean, Cat," he said. "I'm just saying that you're a fighter and you did what you needed to do to survive. I admire that—hell, I know that life all too well," he admitted. Cat sat back and eyed him suspiciously.

"You know my life?" she questioned. "How could you know what it feels like every time I have to show up at a seedy motel and knock on the door, knowing exactly what waits for me on the other side? How could you possibly know how disgusting I feel every time I have to crawl into the backseat of some John's car to give him a blow job or let him use my body? You know me, Repo—really?" she challenged.

"Yes," he breathed. "I've been in your shoe's Cat. You think you're the only person who's had a tough childhood?" he asked.

"No," she whispered. "I'm not that naive, Repo. I've seen sadness and destruction and I know I'm not the only person affected by it. I've told you my sad story—how about you tell me yours?" she asked.

Repo stood and paced the floor in front of the bed and she wondered if he was going to run. She knew what it felt like to be so scared out of your mind that all you could think about was running away. Hell, it was her go-to move and if she wasn't mistaken, Repo had that same wild look in his eyes that she recognized in herself.

"This isn't about me, Cat," he said. "I'm sorry that you've been through hell but I won't go and spill my guts just because you think we're sharing here. That's not what this is —we don't have a give and take relationship going on here," Repo said.

"So, I'm supposed to just give and you take then?" she challenged.

"I wouldn't call posting your bail as me taking anything from you, Cat. How about we just forget the whole thing? You need to get up and get dressed. We're leaving in about thirty minutes," he said. Repo started for the door and Cat panicked.

"Wait—where are you taking me now? You can't just drag me around with you all day. Am I supposed to just be your shadow now?" she asked. Cat knew that the longer Repo kept her tethered to his side, the less her chances were that she'd be able to get free of him. And, that was the plan—running. It was always her plan.

"I'm taking you to my house in Tennessee. I can't trust you to behave yourself here and honestly, I'm tired from staying up all night worrying that you won't try to run again. I can see it in your eyes, Honey. You're thinking about running and if you do that—"

"You're out the money you put up for me," she finished for him. Cat was just a payday for him and she knew it but after she spilled her guts and told him her story, she was hoping that Repo might give her a little more trust. He shouldn't though. He was right not to trust her because she was going to take off just as soon as she saw her opening. If he took her to Tennessee, she wouldn't find that opening and she'd be trapped with him until her arraignment.

"I can't leave the state," she countered. "I have a courtroom to show up to when they call me. If you take me to Tennessee, I won't be able to meet with my court-appointed lawyer."

Repo turned back to look at her and smiled. "I've got it all worked out Cat," he promised. "You are free to travel as long as you don't leave my side. As for your lawyer, I've hired one for you in Tennessee. You'll need someone who knows how to keep you out of prison and I have a friend who was willing to help out."

"You hired a lawyer for me?" she whispered. Repo was surprising her at every turn. One minute he was surly and mean and the next, he was doing something sweet like hiring her a lawyer.

"Yeah," he said. "Now, get your ass out of bed and get dressed—you just wasted five minutes." He walked out of the room, shutting the door behind him and Cat wondered what her next move should be. He wasn't leaving her much choice—she was going to have to go with him to Tennessee and hope that at some point, she would figure out her plan because, for the first time in her life, she didn't have one.

REPO

It only took a half a day for them to get to his cabin in Gatlinburg. He called ahead and had his housekeeper open the house up and stock the fridge so when they got there, he wouldn't have to drag Cat back out for food. She was turning out to be quite a handful but what choice did he have? He needed her to show up for her hearing so he could collect his money. Hell, that wasn't quite true anymore. She had become more than a payday to him. Her story ripped his heart out and that was completely unexpected.

Repo had been around plenty of heartbreak and knew that most of his clients faced hard times that they let define who they became. He wouldn't be the man he was without his jaded past pushing him to become more—be worthy. He just never found who or what he was trying to be worthy for. He wanted to believe it was for his club—Savage Hell. He loved those guys like they were his family. They were the only family he had ever known and he was so thankful for every member—especially his Prez, Savage. He was like a father and brother that Repo never had, all rolled up in one guy. Savage was his best friend and he knew that in a jam, he'd be right by Repo's side if he needed him.

He pulled into the garage of his cabin and cut the engine. "This is me," he said. It didn't matter what Cat thought of his place but—it did. What the fuck was wrong with him? He needed to keep his head on straight and remember that they were at his cabin because of her. Cat was trying to sneak out and meet a client for sex and that wasn't going to change just because he was being stupid. She was a prostitute who got herself in trouble and he wasn't going to be her knight in shining armor riding in to save her. That wasn't who he was—not for Cat or anyone else for that matter.

"It's nice," she said, "for a prison that is," she quickly added. Repo chuckled and got out of his truck, turning back to Cat when she didn't make a move to join him.

"Well, come on and I'll show you to your cell," he teased. She gave him a smirk and hopped out of his truck and stretched. He let his eyes leisurely roam her body and she knew exactly what she was doing. Cat liked the attention and was trying to get his at any cost.

"Cat," he said her name, more as a warning than anything else.

"Fine," she spat, "I'm coming." She grabbed her bag from the front seat and slammed the truck door, following him into his cabin. She looked around and smiled. "Wow," she said, taking in the great room. He wasn't sure why he liked her response but he did.

"Thanks," he said. "Bedrooms are down here," he nodded to the left and she followed behind him. He opened the first door they came to and she walked in, dropping her bag on the king-sized bed.

"I've never slept in a bed this big," she almost whispered.

"Well, it's all yours for the time being. My room is at the end of the hall but just so you know Cat, I have a state of the art surveillance system in the cabin. You even think about leaving and I'll know it."

Cat nodded, "Got it and if I try to run, you'll find me," she said repeating his earlier words to him.

"Exactly," he agreed.

"You honestly don't have to worry about that here, Repo. I have nowhere to go in Tennessee and no one to meet," she admitted.

"We'll see," he taunted. "You seem like a pretty resourceful woman, Cat. I'm betting in just a few days you'll have come up with a new plan to make my existence hell. Let's just try to get through this and we'll be back in Huntsville for your trial before you know it."

"That's comforting," she grumbled. "Listen, I'm tired. Do you mind if I have a nap?" Repo looked her over like he didn't believe her. Honestly, he was on guard constantly around her waiting for whatever scheme she came up with next.

"Sure, Honey," he said. "I could use a nap myself. How about I wake you for dinner later?" he asked.

"Sounds good," she agreed.

"I figured you should have this back," he said, handing her cell phone to her. Repo turned to leave her room, shutting the door behind him. He knew he was taking a chance giving her back her lifeline to her clients but he also knew that she probably didn't know anyone in Tennessee to call. He did it as a show of good faith, letting Cat know that he wasn't such a bad guy.

He was beat and he had just a few things to do before he'd have to make dinner. It was time for him to call back home and fill in Savage. Then, he'd figure out his next move because he honestly didn't have one and he worried that without a plan, Cat would best him and that couldn't happen.

Repo called Savage and filled him in on his location. Of course, his friend asked if he needed back-up and he told him no. He wasn't ready to admit that he couldn't handle his shit. Cat was a handful and the chances of her trying to sneak past him again were pretty good. He promised Savage that he'd call to check in every few days and if he needed help, he'd holler. But, Repo planned on doing everything in his power to make sure that didn't happen.

He walked down the hall to the back bedroom where he

put Cat. Honestly, this wasn't the first time Repo had checked on her under the guise of, "Just wanting to know if she needed anything." If he was reading Cat right, she could see right through all of his excuses, not that it mattered. Not that he'd stop checking in on her to make sure that she hadn't decided to run again. He knew that was ridiculous but nothing about Cat being in his home seemed to make sense.

She made him half-crazy and if he was being completely truthful, he was attracted to her. Hell, every time she walked into the same room with him his dick stood up to take notice of the sexy, curvy blond. And, Lord help him if she didn't start wearing more clothing, he was going to self-combust. Cat had to leave her apartment in a hurry and thanks to her scumbag landlord, she left half her stuff there. There was no way he was going to let her go back to that place and get her stuff and when he offered to do it for her, she all but bit his damn head off. Cat went on for the better part of an hour about not needing a man to take care of her and men being cavemen and only good for one thing. She made his head spin but that's what Cat seemed to do to him—made him horny and pissed off all in one breath. Especially since her new wardrobe consisted of his t-shirts that barely covered her lacy panties that sometimes peeked out at him when she bent over. Yeah—he was a goner.

"Hey," he said, tapping on her door. She left it open since the last time he checked in on her. "You doing all right?" he asked.

"Love of God, Repo," Cat grumbled. "You are driving me

insane." She stood and crossed the room to square off with him. "I'm sure you have something better to do than to check in on me every ten minutes, right?" She put her hands on her curvy hips as if waiting him out. He decided against telling her how hot she looked or the fact that he wasn't checking in on her every ten minutes. It was more like every twenty minutes, but yeah—he'd keep that to himself for his safety.

"You really can't blame me," he said, crowding over Cat's small frame. She was so petite compared to him. "I mean after your great escape plan failed, I figured you'd try again. Am I wrong?" She stared him down, her lips pressed together and God, he wanted to push her up against the bedroom wall and kiss her.

"No," she said, seeming to deflate some with her truth. "I'll probably try to run at every turn. So, why keep me here, Repo?"

"I have no other choice," he breathed. He didn't either.

"That leads me to believe that you're either dumb or a masochist. Which is it?" she questioned.

"Little bit of both," he said. "I don't know what it is about you, Cat, but I can't let you go knowing the type of life you'd be returning to." He didn't mean to sound like he was talking down to her but judging by her expression, it's exactly how she took his comment.

Cat pointed her little finger into his chest and even that seemed to turn him on. He was going to have to get laid soon or he was going to be doomed to fail in his quest to ward sexy little Cat off. "You don't get to judge me or the way that

I was living, Repo," she accused. "How dare you think you're better than me," she shouted. He didn't believe he was better than she was. Hell, maybe that's why he cared so much about keeping her safe with him. He saw her potential but she wasn't ready to hear that from him. His life had been a shit show but telling Cat about his past wouldn't change her mind about him. She'd already decided who he was.

"Can we come to some truce?" he asked.

"Like?" she questioned.

"Well, for starters," he breathed, looking her half-naked body over, "you could wear more in the way of clothing around here." Cat looked down her body and smiled back up at him, giving him a slight shrug.

"I don't see a problem with what I'm wearing, Repo. You want to tell me what's so upsetting about me wearing your t-shirt?" Cat ran her hands down her curves and he damn near swallowed his tongue. The little minx knew exactly what she was doing to him and his will power and she was enjoying every second of teasing him.

"When you bend over in my t-shirt, Honey, I can see those sexy little panties you wear," he taunted. Cat gasped as if she was a blushing schoolgirl and he couldn't help his laugh. "We both know you're not that innocent, Cat and I'm betting you know exactly what you're doing. I'm guessing that you are using me being distracted as part of your plan to take off." Her smile was wicked, telling him he hit his mark.

"As much as I'd love to comply with your request to wear more clothes, Repo, I don't have many to choose from. I have just a few outfits and as for my sleep attire," she said, pointing down her body. "I don't usually wear anything to bed, so this is covering up for me." She grabbed the hem of her t-shirt and started to pull it up her body. He didn't let her get far before he put his hands on her arms, halting her progress.

"Stop," he ordered.

"But, you seem to have a problem with me wearing your clothes. I thought I'd fix our problem and give your shirt back to you," she teased.

"Keep it," he grumbled. "Consider it a gift—I don't care what you call it. Just keep it the fuck on," Repo ordered.

She dropped her hands to her sides, "Suit yourself," she said. "Thanks for the shirt. We done here?" she asked.

"No," he said. "I think we need some ground rules before I try to get some shut-eye," he said. "I didn't sleep well last night."

"What ground rules?" she asked.

"This place is completely monitored and I have cameras that pick up every movement around the perimeter of the house. I also have most rooms under surveillance. So, if you get the stupid idea to take off again, I'll know it before you even hit the property line. And, Cat—you run and I'll find you," he promised. She mimicked his last sentence complete with a whole lot of attitude and stuck her tongue out at him after she finished. He wanted to laugh but now wasn't the time. Cat needed to know that he wasn't screwing around anymore. He was tired and felt about ready to drop and the only way he'd get any rest would be to make her understand the importance of her decisions.

"This place really is a fucking prison," she grumbled. "So, you get a twenty-four, seven peep show—got it," she spat. "Anything else, Warden?"

This time Repo didn't hide his chuckle. He had to admit, he liked his women a little rough around the edges and a whole lot bratty. Cat was both of those things and seeing her so angry only made him want her even more.

"Listen," he barked. "We have about two weeks before you get called back to Huntsville and until that happens, I have no problem enforcing the rules around here. Call me the warden or anything else you like, Honey," he said. "But you will follow my rules."

"Or what?" she questioned.

"Or I'll take you over my knee and spank your ass red," he growled. "Don't fuck with me."

"Okay," she whispered. "How about asshole?" she questioned. He was having trouble keeping up with their conversation.

"Asshole?" he asked.

"Sure," she agreed. "You know—for what I can call you. You said warden worked for you but that I could call you whatever I'd like. Well, I'd like to call you an asshole." He smiled down at her and shook his head at her childish antics.

"I've been called so much worse, Honey," he taunted. "If that's all you can come up with, I'm fine with it. But, you will follow my rules, Cat and you will behave yourself until you have your day in court."

"Fine," she spat. He knew she was done talking to him. Hell, he could feel her anger rolling off her body. He turned to leave her room and looked back in her direction.

"I'm getting a few hours' sleep, Cat. Remember, I'll be watching you, Honey." He walked out of her room and down the hallway to his room.

"Asshole," he heard her grumble just before her door slammed shut. He closed his bedroom door and sprawled out on his king-size bed. First, he needed some sleep and then, he'd finish going over their list of ground rules. He had a feeling he'd need every rule he could think of and then some to deal with his new house guest because she seemed to want to give him hell around every corner.

CAT

Cat had stayed in her room for the rest of the night refusing to even come out for dinner. When Repo knocked on her door and asked if she was hungry, she shouted at him to go the fuck away. He just chuckled and walked away but the joke was on her really because she woke up at the butt crack of dawn starving. Her stomach rumbled for what felt like the millionth time and she knew that if she didn't get up and find some food, she'd never go back to sleep.

She slipped from her warm bed and pulled open her door to peek out into the dark hallway. If she was lucky, she'd be able to sneak down to the kitchen, find something to eat, and get back to her room without running into Repo. She wasn't ready for another showdown and although she didn't know him very well, she knew him enough to know that he'd want another chance to impose some house rules on her and that wasn't her scene. Sure, she was thankful that Repo had given her a safe place to stay—a roof over her head, food in her belly, and the ability to stay off the streets.

Honestly, she wasn't sure how she let her life go so far downhill. There was the whole thing with her step-father but she was one of the lucky ones. She got out of that shitty situation and when she left her mother's house, she vowed to do better for herself. Cat was going to make herself into something more than her old life would have ever allowed but that wasn't what happened—not by a long shot.

When she got to Huntsville, she found an ad in the paper for a sublet. That's when she met Natalie Cassidy. They had similar stories but Nat was all alone in the world. She was physically abused by her father and when both of Nat's parents died in an auto accident, she was on her own. She was eighteen and found a way to land on her feet and that gave Cat so much hope.

Nat became her best friend and she felt comfortable enough to share what had happened to her. Nat helped her find a job at a local diner and she was even being trained to start working in the bakery—something Cat always wanted to do. Nat worked at the bakery and she was so excited about having Cat in there with her. Everyone around town knew them as Cat and Nat—they were inseparable and for years, Cat thought she had found a way to overcome where she came from. She had beaten her shitty past and found a way to happiness. That was all taken away from her when the cops showed up at their apartment to tell her that Nat was gone. She was in a car wreck and was killed instantly and Cat found herself spiraling into the dark depression that had consumed her when she was living back at her mom's house.

Losing Nat felt like she lost a piece of herself and staying in their cheery little apartment felt wrong. Cat moved out and found herself a crappy little efficiency that she could afford by herself and she drank herself half stupid for months. That's about the time that her landlord showed up at her apartment for the first time, threatening to evict her if she didn't pay up one way or another. Cat had lost her job at the diner and had no real job skills to speak of. She applied everywhere in town but things were tough all over and finding a job proved impossible. She did what she had to do and decided not to look back. The money wasn't bad at first. Her clients were generous with their tips and referrals and for a while, she even thought about getting out of that hell hole she was in. But then a pimp named Sly moved in on her territory, putting his girls on every street corner in town and when she refused to go with him, she noticed a decline in business. Yeah, Sly was a real piece of shit and she even thought about giving in and signing on with him but that would mean she'd have to sell her soul to the devil and Cat wasn't about to do that.

Things were so tough she had even thought about just giving up and going home to Maryland but then she'd have to deal with her step-father and that was something she vowed never to do. No, she was better off on her own and that point was driven home every day of her existence because no matter how bad things got for her she could rest easy knowing that at least she wasn't living under the same roof as that predator.

Cat rummaged through the big kitchen for something to eat. She looked into the refrigerator and found a plate that Repo had saved for her, covered in foil with a sticky note with her name on it. She thought it was the sweetest thing anyone had done for her in a damn long time. Cat pulled it from the fridge and popped the foil open to look inside.

"It's chicken," he said from behind her. She straightened to her full height and at only five-three, she had to crane her head to look up at him.

"You made me a plate," she said. She wasn't sure if she was stating a fact or asking him a question.

"I did," he answered. "That okay?"

Cat shrugged as if it wasn't a big deal but it was. "Sure," she said. "Thanks."

"It's not a big deal," Repo said blowing off his sweet gesture. "It's easier to cook for two people than just one," he said.

"I'm not much of a cook," Cat admitted. "I usually didn't have a lot of food in the house to whip something up. Most nights was either a sandwich or a bowl of cereal before I'd head out to work." She removed the foil from the plate and shoved it into the microwave and turned it on. "This looks good though. Do you like to cook?"

"I don't mind," he admitted. "I'm afraid I'm not great at it but I get by. I have a few things I learned to make and the rest I just make up. I watch a lot of cooking shows," he said. He grimaced as if he told her a secret he shouldn't have and she giggled.

"Really?" she questioned. "I wouldn't have pegged you as a lover of cooking shows, Repo."

"Well, let's just keep that between the two of us," he said. Cat pulled the hot plate of food from the microwave and grabbed the fork from the counter where Repo laid it out for her. She shoveled a bite into her mouth not caring that it burned her tongue.

"This is good," she said around a mouthful of food. "How about you keep cooking for me and I'll keep my mouth shut about you watching cooking shows," she offered.

Repo nodded and smiled, "Deal." He pulled out a kitchen chair for her and motioned for her to sit. She walked across the kitchen and sat down in the chair, watching as he sat across from her.

"So, you usually eat dinner at the break of dawn?" he teased.

"I was so hungry I couldn't sleep," she admitted. "Sorry if I woke you."

"You didn't really," he said. "I was up already. I'm an early riser but I was hoping to grab a few more hours sleep."

"Well, I knew that if I didn't get up and feed my growling tummy, I'd never get back to sleep. I hope you don't mind that I helped myself to your fridge." Cat took another bite of food and hummed. "I think you're not giving yourself enough credit, Repo," she gushed. "This is really good."

"Glad you like it," he said. When he smiled at her like he was, Cat could see a different side of him. It was endearing to see Repo a little vulnerable and even somewhat shy. He seemed like a big, badass most of the time and this was a refreshing new side of him.

"I can feel you want to talk about something, Repo—so, let's just have it," Cat said around another mouthful of food.

"We never finished our discussion about rules," Repo said. She knew he had more on his mind earlier but she dismissed him. Cat knew that sooner or later they would circle back around to this issue.

"Fine," she said. "Your house, your rules. Let's have them then, Repo. I'll hear you out while you tell me how to be the perfect houseguest."

"That's not what this is, Cat. I need to know that you aren't going to take off on me again. I told the court that I'd be keeping an eye on you and if you run, I won't be able to show my face in Huntsville again, let alone work in that town. I'm not looking for much from you, Cat. I just need your word that you'll stick around and stop giving me so much trouble. I've got other things I need to focus on and I'd like not to have to worry about you taking off."

Cat barked out her laugh, "Yeah—wouldn't want you worrying about me, Repo. Listen, I have nowhere else to go, so you're stuck with me until my day in court. I will do my best to behave and as for running, I won't."

He stood and held his hand out to her, "I have your

word?" he said. Cat rolled her eyes and took his offered hand.

"Yeah sure," she said. "So dramatic, Repo," she chided.

"Says the woman who tried to sneak out of my apartment in the middle of the night," he reminded. He was never going to let her live that down.

"I have a job in town tomorrow and you'll come with me," he ordered. "Rest up today, sleep as late as you'd like but we leave tomorrow morning at six."

"Six in the morning?" she squeaked.

"Yep," he said.

"But, I promised you that I wouldn't run. Why can't I just stay here?" she questioned.

"Because I don't trust you, Cat. I appreciate you saying you won't run but I will be keeping a close eye on you. I don't know how long I'll be gone on this stakeout and I'm taking you with me."

"A stakeout—like we'll be watching a bad guy and he won't know it?" she asked.

"No," he said, taking her empty plate from in front of her. "I'll be watching a bad guy and you'll be in the car with me. You stay out of my way Cat and we'll get along just fine."

"Which leads me back to my last question—why can't I just stay here?" Repo shook his head at her and smiled.

"Because I said so," he simply said. "I'm getting some more shut-eye. Turn off the lights when you go back to bed," he ordered. Cat slumped into her chair and crossed her arms over her chest. She was pouting but she didn't give a fuck.

Repo knew how to push all her buttons and it was starting to get old.

"Night," he said back over his shoulder. He didn't wait for her to reply, knowing that she wouldn't be giving him one. Yeah—he was testing her last nerve and God help her, he seemed to be enjoying every minute of it.

REPO

Repo had the day practically to himself and he hated it. If he was being honest, he wanted to spend the day with Cat getting to know his sexy little inmate a little better. God, she was his type—sassy, fearless, and sexy as fuck. She had gone back to her room shortly after he went to his master suite. He wasn't lying when he told her he had the whole house rigged with security cameras. He had them all on a feed streaming straight to an app on his phone and every move she made sent his phone an update. The only room in the house that didn't have cameras was her room. He didn't want to seem like a creepy peeping Tom but a part of him wondered what the hell she was doing in there all day.

He heard her shower go on just before dinner time and he decided to take a few minutes and make something nice for her. He didn't mind doing the cooking and honestly, having her compliment his efforts felt good. He had been alone for so long he had forgotten what it was like to have another person relying on him. When he was finally finished making dinner, he softly tapped on her door only to have her bark at him to take a hike again for the second night in a row. Repo wrapped her plate and wrote her name on a sticky note again, putting it in the refrigerator for Cat. He knew that sooner or later, her stomach would win out just like it had earlier that morning and she'd go in search of food. He just wished she'd want to have dinner with him but maybe her way was for the best. At least if she avoided him, he wouldn't have to make small talk or risk the possibility of falling for the blond vixen.

He retired to his room early with his files, wanting to get a jump start on the case for tomorrow. Repo was happy that he was going to get some hours in. In just the few days that Cat was with him, he had given up four cases and a shit ton of cash. He couldn't sit on the sidelines forever and having Cat come with him might be a craptastic idea but it was the only one he had. He just kept reminding himself that this situation wasn't forever and that sooner or later, Cat would be out of his life and he could go back to normal. But, why did that thought make him so unhappy? The idea of things going back to his normal, daily, lonely routine didn't feel as good as he thought it would. Sure, he had Savage Hell but the guys all had their own lives. They were all meeting women and starting families. Hell, even Savage was falling into that category and Repo never thought he'd see the day that his club's Prez would settle down—but he had.

Maybe it was time for him to come up with a new plan—one that had him finding the person he was supposed to spend his life with. Hell, he wouldn't even mind a few kids but he never gave it much thought, too worried he'd end up fucking them up as much as his parents had him. Seeing his buddies with kids made him think about things he never thought he wanted and he had to admit that having Cat under his roof wasn't helping with those crazy dreams. She made him think about things he never allowed himself to hope for. In just a few days, she had started to turn his life upside down and Repo wasn't quite sure how to right it. The only thing he could come up with was that he needed to keep his head on straight, his zipper up, and his hands to himself if he wanted to avoid falling into bed with Cat.

EARLY THE NEXT MORNING, JUST AS HE PROMISED, HE KNOCKED on her door. When she didn't answer, he tried the handle knowing that she liked to lock her door when she slept. He understood that part of her too. His life felt so crazy and dangerous when he lived out on the streets. There were some nights when he used to lay awake and just pray for daylight. At least in the light, he could see what was coming for him. He would have given just about anything to have four walls and a doorknob to lock behind him—keeping him safe. He wondered if Cat had ever felt safe or if she was still afraid even under his roof. A part of him wished he could convince her that nothing bad would happen to her, not on his watch at least. But it would do him no good. She wouldn't believe him if she didn't trust him and from the fear he saw in her beautiful blue eyes every time she stared him down, she didn't believe him at all.

"Cat," he said through the door, pressing his mouth into the corner. "You up?" he could hear her stirring and was thankful he wouldn't need to break into her room again. That ended up being a giant fuck-up on his part and one he wouldn't be repeating.

"Yeah," her sexy, sleepy voice stuttered back. "I'm up. Fuck, Repo what time is it anyway?"

He chuckled to himself, "Five-thirty," he said.

"In the morning?" she asked. "What the hell is wrong with you? Do you have something against sleep?" Yeah, she wasn't thrilled about getting up before the sun but they needed to get moving if he was going to start his surveillance.

"Just get a move on," he ordered. "I need you in the car in twenty." He could hear the long string of curses Cat craftily slurred together and he laughed, walking back to his room. He had already been up for an hour and had a quick workout in the gym he had built in the basement. He liked to start the day with a workout. It helped to calm his nerves and keep him focused throughout the day and with his job, he needed all the focus he could get.

By the time he made his way out to the garage, he found

Cat standing by his pick-up with a piece of toast hanging out of her mouth, a cup of coffee in one hand and a banana in the other. He was shocked that she beat him to the garage but he was hoping that meant she wouldn't be giving him much shit today.

He opened the passenger door for her and she slid in, dropping her banana in her lap and grabbing the toast from her mouth.

"I thought you said to be ready in twenty?" she asked. So much for not giving him shit. He looked her over loving the way she pulled her long, blond hair back into a sleep pony-tail. He made a mental note to talk to Cat about lending her some cash to get some new clothes. She was having to wash the two outfits she owned constantly and he bet she'd welcome a change.

"Why are you looking at me like that, Repo?" she asked. He hadn't realized he was studying her the whole time but he was.

"No reason," he said. "I had a few text messages to return, sorry I'm a little late," he said, hoping his apology would throw her off what he was thinking. He had a feeling Cat wouldn't be thrilled about the fact that he was thinking about how good she looked in her skin-tight jeans or the fact that she felt right not only in his pick-up but his home too.

He shut her door and rounded his truck to the driver's side and hopped in. "So, what are we doing today?" she asked, nibbling at her toast.

"We are going to stake out a client's husband," he said.

"Wait, I thought you were a bail bondsman?" Cat asked.

"Well, that's one of my services. I also run a security agency and have some pretty high profile clients here in town—you know with the whole country music scene? I'm a gun for hire," he said.

"I see that," she said. "It makes sense."

"What do you mean?" Repo asked. Sure, he wasn't the most upstanding citizen but he at least wasn't a thug.

"Don't get all defensive," Cat said. She rested her hand on his arm and didn't make a move to pull it away. "I just meant that you seem like a good person, Repo, and looking out for the good guy, going after the bad guys—well, it fits."

"Thanks," he almost whispered. Repo cleared his throat and smiled over at her. "Well, we don't have far to go today, just around the corner. Hopefully, I'll get the proof that I need that this asshole is cheating on my client. Maybe a few hours tops," he promised.

"Well, that's good because I have a pretty busy schedule," she teased. "When we get home I'm going to need to take a shower and then I'll probably sleep some more—who knows? The sky's the limit." She pulled her hand free from his arm as if she suddenly realized they were still connected. "Sorry," she whispered.

"Not a big deal," he said. "This is the spot." He pulled into a little space between two sedans and parked his truck. "How about you add having dinner with me to your long list of things to do, Cat?" he asked. He watched her as she seemed to weigh her decision and when she smiled up at him, Cat nearly took his breath away.

"All right," she agreed. "Since you asked so nicely."

Repo shook his head at her, "You aren't ever going to make things easy, are you?" Cat mimicked him, shaking head.

"Probably not," she admitted. "I like to keep things interesting."

"You certainly do that," he teased. He pulled out his surveillance gear and got set up. He wasn't kidding with wanting things to go quick and easy today. He was dog tired and the sooner he could prove this asshole was cheating, the sooner he could make them both some dinner and get to bed. He just wished like hell he could talk her into his bed with him but that would be a major rule breaker. And, a major mistake to boot.

THE STAKEOUT TOOK A LITTLE OVER THREE HOURS AND BY THE time they finished, he had enough evidence to present to his client the proof that her husband was not only cheating on her but he was doing so with another woman and a man. The first hour they were there, a woman showed up to the little apartment complex the sleazeball was hauled up in. He had done enough research on the guy to know exactly where he'd be found and it had all panned out.

He got pictures of the woman both coming and going

from his place and then when he was just about to call it a day, a guy showed up. At first, Repo thought it was just a casual business meeting or something. That was until the guy pulled his client's husband in for one of the hottest kisses he'd ever witnessed. Even Cat thought so judging by her, "Wow" comment.

Repo pulled his camera back out from where he had packed it away and started taking pictures, wanting physical proof since he didn't believe what he was seeing. The men disappeared into the apartment and Repo and Cat waited them out. By the time the two men emerged from the apartment and both left in their cars, he had compiled quite a dossier for his client. All that was left was to get home and type everything up to present to her.

They got back to his place and pulled into his garage and he yawned and stretched. "I'm beat," he admitted.

"Me too," Cat said. "I wouldn't mind a hot shower and a nap. I slept for shit last night." She seemed to have a colorful way of putting things and it always made him smile.

"How about we both get some sleep and then I'll wake you for dinner?" he asked.

"Sounds good," she agreed.

"Any requests for dinner?" he asked.

"Nope." She opened her door and jumped out of the truck. "I'll eat just about anything. I told you already, I'm not picky."

He unlocked the door to his house and unarmed his alarm. "I like that about you Cat," he said. "You're so easy going." He rolled his eyes at her and she giggled. "You've been no trouble at all," he added.

"Well, you just have to get to know me a little better, Repo. You might be pleasantly surprised at what you find." He watched as Cat walked right past the kitchen and down the hallway to where her room was, her ass playfully swaying as if she knew he was watching her. Yeah—no trouble at all.

CAT

Cat woke up to the soft tapping at her door and groaned. "I'm up Repo," she grumbled.

"Dinner will be ready in fifteen minutes, Honey. You still hungry?" he asked. He made no move to come into her room and for that, she was thankful. Cat still didn't trust Repo and that had nothing to do with how he had been treating her and everything to do with her issues. Honestly, she didn't trust anyone and that was fucked up.

"I'm starving," she admitted. "I'll come to the kitchen in a few minutes," she said effectively dismissing him.

"Sounds good," he said. She listened for his footsteps to walk away, fading down the hallway before she pulled the covers from her body and stood. She slipped back into the clothes she wore earlier and padded off to the bathroom to brush her teeth and pull her hair back into a braid. Cat checked her reflection in the mirror and studied her sunken eyes and gaunt cheekbones. She had seen better days and her reflection proved that everything she had been through over the past week was taking its toll on her.

"As good as it gets," she mumbled to herself. Cat unlocked her bedroom door and made her way down the hallway to the kitchen to find Repo standing on the other side of the center island, setting the table for two.

"Wow," she breathed. "You didn't have to go to all this trouble." She walked around the counter and stood at the head of the big farm table. Her stomach growled and she looked over the meal he made.

"Jambalaya," he said. "It's just something I found on television and always wanted to try. I guess you gave me an excuse to try something new." He looked her up and down and smiled at her but she could tell that he was checking her out. She had found him looking her over a few times in the last few days and Cat had to admit—it was hot the way he watched her. Still, she knew enough to keep her distance because getting too close to him would be a mistake. Cat was a loner and for good reason. She could never let herself get close to someone again, not like she had Nat. She lost a sister the day Nat died and it hurt like hell, she'd never survive falling in love with someone and losing that person.

"Well, it smells wonderful," she said, clearing the lump of emotion from her throat. Repo pulled her chair out for her and she smiled up at him as she slipped into it. "Thank you," she said.

"Welcome," he returned. "But, you might want to save your thanks until after you taste my jambalaya though. Remember this is the first time I've ever made it and I can't promise it's edible."

Cat giggled, "I'm sure it's fine she said."

"Let's find out," he offered. He sat down next to her and he handed her a bowl of food. Her stomach rumbled again and he chuckled. "Dig in," he said.

She didn't need to be told twice she took a spoonful of jambalaya and shoved it into her mouth. She hummed around the spoonful of goodness and he smiled.

"Really?" he asked.

"So good," she said, shoveling in another bite. "I think you've missed your calling, Repo." He chuckled and took a bite of his food.

"Hey, that is pretty good," he said. "Maybe I'm onto something here. You must inspire me to create new dishes." Repo reached across the table and took her hand into his own and Cat looked down to where he joined their fingers and back up at him. She thought about pulling her hand free but the connection felt nice.

"Repo," she whispered.

"Cat," he returned. "Can't we just have a nice night? I'd like to forget everything else and have a nice evening together. I'm not asking you for anything," he promised.

She leaned into him and God he smelled good. "What if I'm offering you something?" she asked. Cat had never felt so unsure of herself. Hell, she wasn't shy especially when it came to sex. Most of her clients wanted her to take control and call the shots. But, with Repo, she felt unsure and worried that she was overstepping and even misreading his intentions.

"I'm flattered, Cat," he said, pulling his hand from hers. "But, that wouldn't be smart." She pushed her bowl back and stood from her chair.

"I see," she whispered. "It's because of who I am, right? I mean—who wants to fuck a whore?" Repo stood from his chair and reached out for her. She shrugged free from his hold. "Don't," she ordered.

"That's not what I was saying, Cat. I'm not judging you. Hell, I'd never judge you because that would mean I'd have to take a long, hard look at my own life," he said.

"What the hell does that mean, Repo? You keep sending me these crazy mixed signals and I'm so tired of trying to figure out what you want from me," she whispered. She looked around his house, suddenly very aware of the fact that she was in his home and had nowhere to go but all she could think about was running.

"Don't Cat," he barked. "I can see it in your eyes," he warned.

"See what?" she spat. "You think you know me, Repo but you don't. Hell, you just met me a few days ago and whatever you think you know about me is probably just superficial. Nothing about me is real," she insisted.

Repo pulled her against his body and sealed his mouth over hers. He licked and nipped at her lips until she parted them for him to slip his tongue in. She gasped when he grabbed a handful of her ass and squeezed and just when she thought she couldn't possibly take anymore, she broke their kiss, leaving her panting for air.

"Fuck," he spat. "Did that feel real, Cat? You are real and what I'm feeling is real but that doesn't make this a good idea. Hell, it's a fucking awful idea. I need to keep work and pleasure separated and right now—" he paused but she got the jest of what he was going to say next.

"I'm work," she whispered. He gave a curt nod and she turned to run out of the kitchen. She couldn't stand there anymore, not with the way he was looking at her with so much sympathy it made her want to cry for herself. Instead of running back to her room, she headed for the front door. Running was her go-to move and right now, the thought of staying in Repo's house wasn't one she could entertain. She needed to get her head straight and put her walls back in place before she had to face him again. Repo had started to chip away at her well-placed barriers and that was dangerous. She knew it but she still let him kiss her and so help her, if he wanted to kiss her again, she'd allow it. She was a masochist, a traitor to her own heart, and yeah—just plain stupid when it came to how she felt about the big, tattooed biker. The last thing she heard before she slammed the door behind her was Repo shouting her name and reminding her that they had a deal. Well, he could take their fucking deal and shove it up his ass. Fuck their deal and fuck him—she was going for a walk to clear her head and decide her next move.

SHE HAD WALKED FOR HOURS AND STILL WASN'T SURE WHAT TO do next. Her only real option was to go back to Repo's house. Her few earthly belongings were at his place—her wallet and phone and box of things. She had to at least return to his house for her stuff but more than that, she had nowhere else to go, although she hated to admit it. She needed Repo and that pissed her off. She never wanted to rely on anyone—especially a man. It wasn't who she was but all her shit finally hit the fan and here she was, fully dependent on a man she barely knew.

She snuck into the house, quietly shutting the front door behind her and locking it. "Where have you been," Repo growled from a chair in the corner of the darkroom. She really couldn't see him but if she could, Cat was pretty sure she'd find one very pissed-off man sitting in that seat. She could almost feel his anger from across the damn room.

"I went for a walk," she said, defiantly raising her chin. "You did say that this wasn't a prison."

"No," he said, standing from his chair. "I never called it a prison—you did and I just never corrected you. We had a deal, Cat," he reminded. "You said you would behave and stop running."

She shrugged, "I guess old habits are hard to break.

Besides, I told you I just went for a walk—so technically not running." Repo was standing so close to her she could smell the whiskey on his breath and it made her stomach revolt. Her step-father used to get drunk before coming into her room at night. His drink of choice was whiskey too and just the stench of it made her want to vomit.

"Have you been drinking?" she asked. Cat sounded more like she was hurling accusations at him. She wasn't his mother or his girlfriend and he could do whatever he wanted. Still, she knew that most men were mean when they were drunk and she took a step back from him.

"So what?" he asked. "What did you think was going to happen, Cat? You think I'd run after you and pledge my undying love to you?" Cat took another step back from him. His words hurt her but she'd never tell him that. She learned a long time ago that fairytales don't exist. She didn't expect him or anyone else to swoop in and save her tonight. She could just save herself.

"Don't flatter yourself, Repo," she spat. "I was just trying to be nice to you earlier. You took me in and gave me a place to land. Consider my gesture payback."

He pointed his finger at her, "I told you the day we met and I'll say it again—you can't pay back your debt with me by offering me sex."

Cat nodded and turned to go back to her room. She wanted to lock herself away and take a hot bath to forget the fact that she had ever met Repo. "Understood," she said back over her shoulder. "Tonight was the last time you'll ever hear me make you that offer again, Repo. You want things to be strictly business and I couldn't agree more. That's how things will remain from here on out." She slammed her bedroom door like a child and quickly locked it. She listened for any movement outside her door and when she heard Repo's heavy boots clomping down the hallway, she held her breath expecting another showdown—but there wasn't one. He kept on walking straight back to his room and slammed his door just as she had.

"Shit," she whispered to herself. She swiped at the hot tears that spilled down her face. "What next?" she murmured. The question had a simple answer. What was next for her wasn't something she could control. Her only options were to avoid Repo at all costs until her court-appointed lawyer called with an update. Then, she'd face her very own judgment day and pray that she came out the other side unscathed.

Cat slept in late the next morning and when she finally emerged from her room into the quiet house, she found it empty. She cautiously tiptoed down to the kitchen, not truly believing her good fortune, and found a note from Repo and read it out loud.

Hey,

I got another gig that will pull me away for a few nights. Stay put—the house is yours. Help yourself to the food in the fridge and

I've left a few take out menus just in case. I've also left the number for my attorney. He's good and can probably help you get a reduced sentence. Just call him and set something up.

Sorry about last night.

Repo

That was it? Just one line about being sorry about last night? Did he expect her to forgive and forget the way he talked to her as if she was an object and not a fucking person? He could just forget it because that wouldn't be happening any time soon. She found the business card he left with his lawyer's contact information and turned it over in her hands. Did she want to be more in debt to Repo? Using his lawyer would only make her feel like she owed him more and that was the last thing she needed right now. She tossed the card up onto the countertop and decided to make herself some scrambled eggs and toast. After last night's little fiasco at dinner, she didn't get much to eat. Walking for miles didn't help her protesting tummy and by the time she had her showdown with Repo, she was starving again.

She picked up his note and re-read it one more time. Where had he gone? He wasn't much on specifics and gave her no clue as to where he'd taken off to. He was probably keeping tabs on her through his security cameras and if she was being truthful, staying at his cabin and having it all to herself wasn't such a bad deal. She used to dream of living in places like his home and now she could have a piece of that fantasy, even if it was going to be short-lived.

She made breakfast and cleaned up after herself and

decided to start a load of her laundry. With just a few outfits to her name, she had to constantly do laundry. When she got back on her feet, the first thing she was going to do was to buy herself a few new outfits. But, that was going to take some time and patience. First, she'd need to find a place to live. That would also depend on if she ended up in prison or not in the next couple of weeks.

Her phone chimed and she almost didn't want to look to see which client was texting her. She squinted at her phone screen, being a complete chicken and not wanting to look at it when she realized the text was from Repo.

You get my note?

She debated whether or not she wanted to answer him back but she also knew that if she didn't, he'd go the extra mile and call her. She didn't want to hear his sexy, gravelly voice. Especially not so soon after he hurt her with the nasty things he said to her.

Yeah.

There, he had his answer. She got his note and she answered his text. Done.

I'm going to be gone a little longer than I originally planned. You good for about a week?

She wanted to text back that she wouldn't be but he'd probably think she was just being coy. The thought of being completely alone for a full week terrified her. It's one of the reasons she took on so many clients. Sure, they might be using her body but she at least had some human contact that living alone never afforded her.

Sure.

Yeah, she lied but telling him that she was a giant pussy too afraid to be alone with her own company wasn't going to happen either.

Later.

Yeah, later.

She sent her last text and turned off her cell, tossing it to her bed. She looked around the room and sighed. A whole week of being alone—just her and the inner dialog that liked to remind her of all her failures. It was going to be one long fucking week, that was for sure.

REPO

Repo was away from home for the better part of the week. He knew he was giving up time with Cat—time he'd never get back with her but judging by the way they left things, maybe that was for the best. He texted her every night and her replies were always curt and to the point. He hated that he had ruined what little relationship the two of them were building. He was beginning to think of her as a friend. Hell, he was beginning to think of her as so much more but admitting that now was pointless.

Tonight, he was going to go home partly because he was sick of being on the road and partly because he wanted to see the woman who was taking up residence in his house. Last night, she texted him that her court-appointed lawyer had reached out to her and they had to travel back to Huntsville in two and a half days and he wanted to make sure she was ready. Of course, he didn't tell Cat that he was on his way home and that in just a few minutes, they'd be face to face again. He worried that if he told her that bit of information, she'd likely take off and he didn't have any more time or energy for games.

His assignment had been one from hell and he worried that he'd never track down the asshole who skipped bail but when he did finally catch up with him, he'd be a very rich man. There was a million-dollar delivery fee if Repo brought him in and that was the plan. He could move back to his cabin full time and put down some roots—something he had always been wanting. After he drove Cat-back to Huntsville for her trial, he was going to help himself forget her by turning around and heading right back to his place in Tennessee. He had a feeling that she'd haunt him even there and that was something he'd have to get used to.

He pulled into his garage and parked his truck. It felt like he had been gone for months and not just days. Repo stood and stretched from his long drive, grabbing his bag from the back of the cab. He walked through the house and dropped his things in the kitchen on the table.

"Cat," he called. The house was quiet and most of the lights were off except for the light coming from down the hall from his master suite. He walked down to his bedroom and peeked inside, still not finding her.

"Cat, you here?" he shouted. Still no answer. He looked around his room and worried that he was too late and Cat had run but that didn't make any sense. He had texted with her earlier that morning and his security cameras hadn't sent him an alert about her leaving.

"Cat," he shouted. He heard some sloshing around in his bathroom followed by Cat's muttered curses. Repo followed the trail of swear words back to his master bath and found her splashing around, trying to get out of the tub—wet and naked.

"Repo," she shouted. "What are you doing here?" He didn't make a move to leave. Honestly, he wasn't sure he'd be able to get his legs to go.

He cocked an eyebrow at her, "I live here, Cat. You want to tell me what you're doing in my bathtub?" He decided to leave out the part where he admitted that she looked damn good in his space. Judging from the angry scowl on her beautiful face, she wasn't going to buy into his cheesy line.

She reached for her towel and he handed it to her. Repo couldn't take his eyes off her body, the way she moved and her perfect, full breasts. The soapy bubbles slid down her sleek belly and for just a minute, he wished he was those damn bubbles. Cat slid her towel around her body and stepped free from the tub, bending over to show off her glorious ass as she pulled the plug to let the water drain. She straightened when she realized he was checking out her ass.

"I mean," she said, clearing her throat to get his attention. "Why are you home? I thought you said you had a couple more days when we texted this morning."

"I did," he said. "But, you will need a ride back to Huntsville in two days and well, I thought—"

"You thought you'd come back and deliver me personally? You wouldn't want to miss out on that bail money, right?" she spat. He wanted to tell her that he didn't need the little bit of money he'd get back from delivering her to court. Hell, he had money in the bank and this new job could set him up for life. Cat was so completely fixated on being right, she'd never listen to his truth.

"That isn't why I came back here early, Cat. I thought we could spend the last two days hanging out before I take you home. I thought I'd do the right thing here, Honey," he growled.

"You wouldn't know the right thing if it bit you in the ass, Repo," she sassed. "I tried to get to know you before you left and you shoved me to the side. God, do you know how that made me feel? How I felt when you treated me like dirt?" A small sob broke through her defenses and he reached for her.

"Cat," Repo whispered.

"No," she shouted. "Don't touch me, Repo. I get it now and I got it then—you don't want me."

"Wanting you isn't the problem, Cat. I thought we were becoming friends here, Honey."

"What we are has nothing to do with friendship, Repo. I'm a job for you, remember?" Cat tightened her towel around her body. "I'm sorry that I used your tub, Repo. I'll clean up after myself and get out of your hair."

"How about I order us some take out?" he asked.

"Not hungry," she said. She picked up her dirty clothes and brushed past him, not looking at him.

"You have to eat," he said.

She spun around and finally looked up at him. "You know what, Repo? I've been here by myself for almost a week now and I didn't manage to forget to eat. I didn't starve to death and I think I can still take care of myself." She turned back around and stomped out of his room and back to hers down the hall, slamming the door behind herself.

"Fuck," he spat. Yeah—that was a shit show. They went from a friendly conversation via text messages to her slamming doors and shouting at him. She was putting her walls back up and there was nothing he could do about it except take her home to Huntsville in a couple of days and wish her the best—whatever that might be.

THE DRIVE BACK TO HUNTSVILLE WAS ALMOST AS PAINFUL AS the past two days spent with Cat in his cabin. She all but disappeared into her room and only came out for food and to do her laundry. Repo had called ahead before they left that morning to tell Savage that he was going to be into the club tonight for church but that he wouldn't be staying in town because of the damn case. He was going to have to head back to Gatlinburg to track down his bail bond runner and then he'd get his shit together to decide what to do next with his life.

He pulled into the courthouse parking lot and Cat unbuckled her seat belt. "You can just drop me off at the door," she offered. "No need for you to come in. I mean—we're done here now, right? Isn't that how this works? I show up and you get your money back. So, you should go and collect that. Thanks for letting me stay at your place, Repo. I appreciate everything."

"Cat—stop," he ordered as she grabbed her box from the back seat.

"Can't," she said. "I'm already late, Repo. I can't risk being held in contempt of court on top of everything else." He knew she was still pissed that he refused to head back to Huntsville with her last night. She asked him to make the drive yesterday instead of this morning and honestly, she wasn't wrong about the traffic that they'd be up against.

"I told you that I was sorry about that about five times in the past hour, Cat. Jesus woman," he growled. "Do you ever just forgive and forget?"

"Oh, I forgive," she said. Her sweet smile didn't quite match her tone. "But, I don't easily forget."

"Fine," Repo barked. "Suit yourself, Cat. But since we're just doing whatever the hell we want here—I'm going to be coming into that courtroom."

"But, that's not necessary," she protested. Cat clutched her box with all her belongings to her chest as if it was her only lifeline. God, he wished she'd let him in. He wanted to be done with them dancing around each other but when Cat pushed him away after he got home the other night, he realized that she didn't feel the same way. He wanted to tell her that he wanted a chance with her but he wouldn't beg. That wasn't Repo's speed.

"Don't care," he said. "Like you said, I need to come in to collect my bond money, so I might as well get a show out of all this. You owe me at least that, right?"

"You know what, Repo?" Cat spat. She looked around the almost empty parking lot and slipped out of his truck. He wondered if she was going to finish what she started saying until she looked back into his pick-up where he sat watching her.

"Go fuck yourself," she said and slammed the passenger door. Repo chuckled to himself and shook his head. She was the most stubborn, determined woman he'd ever met and he had to admit, he was going to miss spending time with Cat Linz but keeping her would be a fucking disaster and he didn't do messy.

CAT

Cat wasn't quite sure what to expect when she walked into the courtroom this morning but finding her court-appointed lawyer very pregnant and barely able to stand without a little help, wasn't even close to what she had in mind. She got to the courthouse with just minutes to spare before her case, thanks to their flat tire and road trip from hell. She wished Repo would have listened to her when she all but begged him to return to Huntsville the night before her hearing. Now, she was rushed and felt completely out of her comfort zone. Not that going to court to plead guilty for prostitution was comfortable to her in any way. But what choice did she have?

She had only spoken to her lawyer once by phone and the woman quickly went over what her options were. In short—

there weren't any. And, the fact that her lawyer was pregnant and probably close to term wasn't even mentioned.

"Hi Catrina," the woman said, pushing herself up from her seat in the back of the courtroom. "I'm Mindy Waters, your attorney."

Cat looked her giant belly over and took the woman's offered hand. "Catrina Linz," she said. "You look about ready to pop," she quickly added.

"Yeah," her lawyer said, pulling her hand free to rub her belly. "I'm due in three more days," she admitted.

"Wow," Cat said. "You're still working?"

Mindy nodded, "Yep," she said proudly. "Sure beats sitting around to watch my ankles swell. You have kids, Catrina?" she asked. The thought of having a kid both intrigued her and horrified her all at the same time. She wanted kids but she was in no way ready to have that kind of responsibility in her life yet. Hell, she technically didn't even have a roof over her head and if it wasn't for Repo, she'd be living out on the street.

"Please, call me Cat. And, no—no kids," she said.

"Well, that's one less problem to worry about for us then. You don't want to have to find accommodations for them if things here go south. Are you ready? Do you have any questions for me?" Mindy asked. Cat had plenty of questions but most of them could be answered with just one.

"Will I do time?" she whispered.

"I'm hoping not but ultimately, that will be up to the

judge presiding over your case. Unfortunately, you got judge Collins and he's tough," her lawyer said.

"Shit," Cat swore under her breath. Repo walked into the courtroom and took a seat on the other side of the room in the back corner. He barely even looked at her and Cat felt a little disappointed that he was treating her like a job again. She was hoping after their time together he'd at least think of her as a friend. Hell, she wanted him to think of her as so much more than a fucking friend but she knew better than to go there with Repo. He had made it crystal clear that he didn't want her. Cat was confident that he was even somewhat repulsed by what she did for a living but that wasn't something she could change anytime soon. She was a twenty-seven-year-old high school drop out with little to no job skills. There was no time to get her GED or on the job training to better her position in life—she was stuck and doing the best she could. If Repo couldn't understand that then that was on him.

"You know that guy?" her lawyer asked. She looked Repo over and shivered. Cat couldn't blame her—he looked pretty menacing sitting there in his black t-shirt that barely covered his sleeves of tattoos that she knew also ran up most of his torso. His hair was past due for a haircut and his scowl told everyone around him to, "Stay the fuck away from him."

"Yes," Cat breathed. "He's my bail bondsman and apparently, my official bodyguard." Cat huffed out a breath and her lawyer giggled, holding her big belly.

"You seem put out by him and I'd give just about anything

to have him guarding my body," Mindy said. Cat looked at her as if she was appalled and her lawyer shrugged. "Don't blame me—it's the crazy pregnancy hormones." Mindy cleared her throat and nodded. "Sorry. How about we go over your plea one more time?"

"Sure," Cat said. They sat down in the back of the courtroom. "Tell me why you think I should plead guilty again," Cat asked. "I don't see how admitting that I committed a crime is going to help my case. Isn't it your job to prove that I'm innocent?"

"Yes," Mindy agreed. "But in this case, we're dealing with a judge who lives in a world of absolutes. He likes his cases black and white. If we go up there and waste his time, it will only piss him off." Mindy nodded to the front of the courtroom and for the first time since being arrested, Cat felt nervous and anxious about what was going to come next.

"So, if we go up there and tell the truth, he'll go easier on me?" Cat asked.

"That's the plan, Cat," her lawyer said. The courtroom started to fill with people and Cat noticed a man in a uniform come in through the side door. He called the room to order and announced the judge who walked into the room in his dark robe and took his seat at the head of the courtroom.

He looked at the man in the guard uniform who had introduced him. "Bailiff call the first case, please," he ordered. The man nodded to the judge and the bailiff called Cat's name.

"Here we go," Mindy said, trying to stand from her seat. Cat held out her hand, offering her some help and her lawyer smiled up at her. "Thanks," she said.

"No problem," Cat whispered. She pulled the woman from her chair and the judge cleared his throat.

"Anytime now, Council," he barked.

"Yes, your Honor," Mindy said. She groaned and wrapped her arms around her belly, doubling over.

"You all right?" Cat asked. She chanced a look back at Repo and he seemed just as concerned as she felt.

"No," Mindy loudly whispered. "I think my water just broke."

"Oh my God," Cat whispered. "What do I do?" Mindy pulled out her cell phone and made a quick call.

"It's time, Babe. You know what to do," she said. Mindy ended the call, "Help me to the front?" she asked.

"Of course," Cat offered. She helped her lawyer to the front of the courtroom and before they even got to the desk where they were both to be seated, Mindy doubled over again in pain.

"Your Honor," Mindy groaned. "I'm afraid I 'm going to need to ask for a postponement."

"And why would you need more time Council?" he asked.

"My water just broke," Mindy said. "You might also want to call in maintenance." She looked back to where her amniotic fluids still lay on the courtroom floor and made a face that Cat wanted to laugh at. "Sorry," she grumbled.

"You're in labor?" the judge asked, still trying to catch up.

"Yes, your Honor," Mindy agreed. She doubled over again in pain, holding onto the heavy wooden desk. Cat noted how her knuckles turned white from her death grip on the table and she felt bad for the woman. "And, judging by how fast these contractions are coming, I'd say that someone needs to call an ambulance because I'm pretty sure I won't make it to the hospital on time."

"Oh God," Cat whispered.

"In light of the current circumstances, I'd say that a postponement is in order. Miss Linz, you will return to this courtroom for another hearing when new council can be appointed for you. Do you have any questions?" the judge asked.

"Yes," Cat stuttered. "Has anyone called an ambulance for this poor woman?" Mindy chuckled and slumped into one of the chairs behind the desk.

"I'm sorry," her lawyer said. "I was hoping that I could help you."

"Me too," Cat said, reaching down to hold her hand. If she was going to have to wait out the ambulance's arrival, the least Cat could do was hold her hand. "But, it looks like you have your hands full—or at least you will, soon enough. I'll be fine," Cat lied. EMTs stormed into the courtroom and Cat immediately moved out of their way so they could attend to Mindy. They got her up and strapped onto the stretcher in no time and she smiled and nodded to Cat.

"Good luck, Cat," Mindy said.

"You too," Cat offered. She followed the EMT's to the

back of the courtroom, holding the door for them. Cat was at a loss as to what she was supposed to do next. Nothing about today had gone as planned and now, she needed to figure out her next move. She was still homeless and was pretty sure she had outlived her stay at Repo's. He spent the morning grumpy and pissed at the world and she knew that had everything to do with his eagerness to be rid of her. She was an unwanted houseguest and she couldn't blame him for wanting to get on with his life. He had things to do and working from his home in Gatlinburg had to put a crimp in his plans.

"Order," the Judge shouted, hitting his gavel on his desk. "Okay, shows over," he said. "I'll see you soon, Miss Linz," he promised. She quietly nodded and left the courtroom, wishing she could run and hide. Today's shitshow was more than she felt she could handle. She was hoping for an end to this nightmare but instead, she was going to have to go through the whole ordeal again.

Cat slumped against the wall in the corner and tried to think through her options. Repo stepped from the courtroom and looked around the lobby and for just a minute, she wondered if he was worried she took off because he'd be out bond money or because he cared for her. No—she couldn't let herself believe in that fairy tale, not again.

"Let's go, Cat," Repo ordered, taking her arm in his big hand.

"Wait, what?" she asked. "You did your job, Repo. You got me here for my court date."

"Right, and now that it's been postponed, so has our goodbyes. I'd say we have another two weeks together before they send you another court date. That means that you're coming home with me again," Repo said. He pulled her along with him and Cat found it nearly impossible to keep up with him.

"You can't just keep me locked up at your cabin forever, Repo," she challenged. "I'll show back up here when I'm summoned and you'll get your money."

"And, I know that how?" Repo asked. "We've already established that you're a flight risk," he challenged.

Cat shrugged, "Let's just say I've had an epiphany," she sassed. She was practically running to keep up with him and he smiled back at her.

"Liar," he challenged. "Have I been that horrible to be around, Cat? I mean, I thought we were getting along. You're starting to hurt my feelings acting as though you don't want to come back home with me," he taunted.

Cat pulled her arm free from his hold. They were just about to his truck in the parking lot but she wasn't about to let him talk to her like that. "You think we've been getting along?" she asked. "How can you say that, Repo? You've treated me like a pest you can't wait to get rid of. Hell, you practically tossed me out of your truck when we got here today, you were so happy to be getting rid of me."

"That's bullshit," he shouted. "I don't want to get rid of you, Cat. I want for this all to be over."

Cat barked out her laugh. They were finally getting

somewhere. At least he was being honest now. "I get it, Repo. You want this whole shitshow over with so you can dump my ass in prison and get on with your life. Well, that's fine by me," she spat. "Honestly, I can't blame you for wanting to be rid of me."

"Rid of you? I thought I just told you that I don't want that, Cat. Hell, I'm trying to figure out a way to fucking keep you but you're so set and determined to run away from me, that's proving impossible," Repo grumbled.

"Keep me?" Cat whispered. She felt like her world was spinning a little faster at his admission. "For the money?" she asked.

Repo shook his head, "Fuck the money," he growled. "Come back to my cabin with me, Cat," he said. This time he sounded less like he was giving her an order and more like he was issuing a plea. Cat looked up into his eyes and God, she wanted to believe that he was asking her to do what she hoped. Did Repo mean to give her a choice in the matter?

"If I agree, what does that mean, Repo," she asked.

"It means that you are agreeing to stop being a pain in my ass, Cat," he said. "It means that you will stop trying to run every time I turn my fucking back. It means that you agree to be mine," he whispered.

"Yours?" she murmured. He leaned over her body and his lips were so close she could feel his breath on her skin.

"Mine," he said. "Tell me yes, Cat," he begged. How could she deny him? The answer was simple, she couldn't.

REPO

Repo felt as though he was holding his damn breath waiting for Cat to give him her agreement and God when she gave him a simple nod, he grabbed her hand and dragged her to his truck.

"Get in," he ordered. Cat looked at him as if he lost his mind.

"I'm not sure if you're happy with my agreement or if I've pissed you off again, Repo," Cat insisted. "You're confusing me." Honestly, he was just as confused about all of this himself. He was royally fucking this all up but he wasn't sure how else to handle what was happening between the two of them.

"Sorry," he breathed. He helped her into the passenger side of his truck and tucked a strand of her blond hair back from her face. "I'm just as confused about all of this, Honey. I'm pissed off at myself, really," he admitted.

"For what?" she questioned.

"For wanting you when I shouldn't. I'm breaking my number one rule by asking you to be mine," he said. "Hell, I've never gotten involved with a job."

Cat giggled, "Well, I can one-up you there, Repo. I've never gotten involved with anyone period."

"Wait, what?" he asked. "You've never had a boyfriend or any type of relationship?" He knew she was twenty-seven from the paperwork he had her fill out after her arrest. How had she gone her whole life and never been in a relationship of any type?

"I told you about my step-father. Once I left home at sixteen, I was living on the streets. That makes it a little tricky to date. Honestly, there aren't many men who want to date a homeless sixteen-year-old girl, you know. I started prostituting myself out and that put a damper on the number of guys who wanted to take me out on a date. So, here we are," she said, holding her arms wide to drive her point home.

"Sorry," he said. "I guess I didn't think through my question before asking it. If it makes you feel any better, I don't do relationships either. Hell, my life hasn't been much different from yours and I've been avoiding anything serious my whole damn life," he admitted. He never wanted to get involved with any one person for too long. The idea of being strapped down to just one person used to scare the shit out of him but since meeting Cat—all that fear seemed to disappear for him. He just hadn't realized it until that morning.

Having to drive her back to Huntsville, worrying about what her future held, made him realize that all the feelings he had been fighting weren't going to just disappear once he was rid of Cat. The thought of having to leave her at the courthouse to be processed and thrown behind bars pissed him off and he found himself putting up his walls to shut her out. That was easier than having to deal with the wave of feelings and emotions that seemed to crash into him, knocking him on his ass. Sure, he wanted this all to be over for her but when that lawyer's water broke and she went into labor, Repo said a little prayer of thanks to the universe. This would give him more time with Cat—more time to figure out what she was coming to mean to him. More time to make her his. That's what he wanted and denying it any longer wasn't something he could do.

"How about we try to figure this out as we go," he said. "I'll try to be less of a grumpy ass and you promise to stick around and give me a shot." Cat looked down at where their hands were joined and back up at him.

"What happens if I end up having to go away?" she asked.

Repo shrugged, "We'll figure that out later then," he promised. "How about we just take this one day at a time?"

"All right," she agreed. Repo leaned in and hesitated, not sure if they were ready for this next step. Hell, he was sure they weren't ever going to be ready for what he wanted to do next but he was done with waiting for a sign or some dumb shit like that. Cat nodded and wrapped her arms around his shoulders.

"You can kiss me, Repo," she said. "If you want to."

"I fucking want to," he growled. Repo dipped his head and kissed her and God, she tasted right. He let his tongue slide into her mouth and she moaned into his. He broke the kiss leaving them both breathless. "So fucking right," he whispered.

"As much as I hate to say this, we need to get going, Honey," he insisted. "I've called Savage and he's waiting over at the bar. We'll stay in town tonight since I have some club business to attend. Will you go back to my cabin with me tomorrow?" he asked.

"You don't have to drag me back to Tennessee, Repo. I promise not to run. When I give my word, I keep it," she said. He believed that about her too, but he wanted to take her back to his home. For some reason, having her in his space felt right.

"I know—just come back to Gatlinburg with me, Cat," he asked.

She nodded, "All right," she said. "I love your cabin, Repo. I'll go back home with you."

"Thank you, Cat," he said.

CAT

Cat was still trying to catch her breath since that scorching kiss with Repo. Her mind was still reeling over the fact that he admitted that he wanted her. It had been two very long weeks of him denying her and leaving her half-crazy with lust. Now, all she had to do was promise him that she'd stop trying to run and she could have the man who made her want things she never thought she would. She could do that—not run. Sure, she was built to take off at the first sign of trouble but she wasn't about to break her promise to Repo. Not after he was so honest with her—she owed him at least that.

"You sure you're up for a quick trip into Savage Hell?" he asked. "I know it's been a long day for you." She wanted to tell him that she was ready to go back to his apartment and pick up where their kiss left off but she had a feeling that tonight was important to Repo. Plus, she had to admit that she was curious about his MC and the men that he called back home to talk to daily. They seemed more like Repo's family and from the little bit that he had shared about himself—he didn't have much family. He seemed to be just as alone in the world as she was and that thought made her heart hurt for him.

"No, I'd like to see where your club meets," she said. "It will be nice to see that side of your life," she admitted.

"It's not a big deal," Repo said, shrugging. "I mean, the guys are all great but it's just a club." She knew he was playing off how important the men in his MC were to him. It seemed that every step forward they took, he pushed her back two steps.

"You don't have to hide how important they are to you, Repo. You call home every day to talk to them and I can tell that they mean something to you. Is that so bad?" she asked.

"The guys are great," Repo defended. "I just don't go and get all mushy about shit," he admitted.

Cat giggled and shook her head, "You're a puzzle, Repo," she said.

"Well," he breathed reaching across the console of his truck to pull her hand into his own. "I'll let you put the pieces together later if you play your cards right," he teased. Cat knew that he was expecting a response but she honestly had none. She wasn't sure how to respond to his outrageous remarks. They were such a one-eighty from how he had been treating her and she wasn't sure that rushing things between them was the answer either.

"We should take things slow," she said. Repo immediately pulled his hand free from hers and she worried that she had said the wrong thing. "This is just so confusing to me, Repo. I mean, you just spent the past two weeks pushing me away and making me feel like you hated me, most days. Hell, I was sure that you couldn't wait to be rid of me and now, all of the sudden today, you want me—just like that?" she questioned.

"Yeah," he breathed. "Just like that, Cat. I fought wanting you because I was following my damn rules. I tried to treat you like a job and ignore the way you made me feel. Hell, you drove me crazy and I didn't have a fucking clue what to do about it all," Repo said.

"What changed?" she asked.

Repo shrugged, "Don't know, really," he admitted. "I guess I'm just done denying what I want. I want you, Cat." She silently watched the landscape pass by her passenger window and he reached back across the console and took her hand into his again. "Still want to take things slowly?" he asked.

"Truth?" she asked.

"Truth," he agreed.

"The idea of you and me scares the shit out of me, Repo. In my line of work, I don't let myself get attached—you know occupational hazards and all that. I keep my clients at arms-length and that works for me," she said. Cat learned long ago to never get involved with her clients. It kept her safe. It helped her to stay sane and find a way to wake up every morning and live with her decisions from the night before.

"I'm not one of your fucking clients," Repo spat. "Is that all you're looking for here, Cat? Are you still hoping to pay me back for your bail bond and then what—just walk away from me?" His accusation felt like a slap and all she could do was stutter her denials.

"It's not like that, Repo. Not anymore," she admitted. "When we first met, I was desperate to run. Hell, I made you that offer because I was hoping to get rid of you so that I could take off. If you had your payment, I'd be able to leave in good conscious."

"I knew you were going to run, Cat," he accused.

She held up her hand effectively stopping his next words. "Let me finish Repo," she insisted. He nodded and she took a deep breath. "But then you took me in and gave me a place to stay. I wasn't sure how to respond to such kindness. No one had ever done anything like that for me," she whispered. Cat looked out her window again trying to get her emotions under control. Repo pulled into a parking lot and parked behind a bar she assumed was Savage Hell. He cut the engine and turned to her giving Cat his full attention. She wasn't sure she'd be able to finish what she needed to say with him watching her. It was hard enough to get it all out with him paying attention to his driving.

"I wanted to believe that you cared. Hell, I was so desperate to think that you wanted me—you know, really wanted me. But then when I practically threw myself at you and you turned me down, time after time, I gave up hope. I thought today was going to be our last day together, Repo. I wrapped my brain around the fact that I was going to walk out of that courthouse alone or worse-I'd end up in prison. But, I never thought that I'd walk out of that place with you by my side or sitting here holding my hand telling me that you want me. So, yeah—I was going to run but I made you a promise, Repo, and I'm not going anywhere. You're just going to have to give my mind a minute to catch up to where my heart's been for a couple of weeks now."

Repo pulled her hand up to his mouth and turned it over, gently pressing his lips to her palm and it was the sweetest fucking gesture she'd ever experienced. "I can take this as slowly as you need, Honey," Repo said. "Go ahead and do all the catching up you need and I'll be right here. I'm not sorry about the way things turned out. I wish this could be over for you but I'm so damn thankful for this second chance."

"Really?" she questioned.

"Yes, really," he said. "I acted like an ass earlier today. Hell, I've been acting like an ass for the past two weeks. I wanted you since the first time I saw you but I let my stupid, self-imposed rules get in the way. I was worried that once today was over I'd be watching you walk away from me and that thought had me crazy. It's why I insisted we spend last night at my cabin—I wanted more time with you and now I have it."

"Sure, until they find another lawyer for me and call me

back into court. You know this could all still end with me ending up in prison, right?" she asked.

"Use the lawyer I found for you," he said. "The one you told me you couldn't use because you'd feel that you owe me again. He said he'd be able to get you community service and no jail time." The idea of getting no jail time was a dream and she didn't want to let herself hope for that.

"What happens if he can't get me off?" she asked.

"Let him at least try, Cat. If not for yourself then for me," he begged. How could she refuse him when he looked at her the way he was?

"All right," she agreed. "But I'm going to pay you back," she insisted.

"No, you won't," Repo said.

"You can't keep on doing shit for me for free, Repo. Sooner or later, I'm going to have to earn my keep," she insisted.

"All right," Repo said. "You have any job skills?" She shot him a smirk, telling him in no uncertain terms that she didn't.

"I dropped out of high school when I was sixteen and ran away. I never got my GED and my job skills, as you like to call them, consist of blow jobs and various sexual positions." Repo looked her over, not at all shocked by what she was saying. She was going for that too—the shock factor but it was as if he hadn't even heard her.

"I know you're trying to get a reaction out of me, Cat but you'll quickly learn that I'm pretty hard to shock. You'd be surprised to know that you and I are very much alike," he said. This was the second time that Repo hinted to his past and she had to admit, she was intrigued.

"How so?" she asked, hoping that he'd finally share. Repo looked at the bar that filled most of the parking lot and then back at her.

"That's a story for another time—promise," he said. "I don't want to go into my past right now. And, stop trying to change the subject. We're talking about your job skills and not my past."

"Actually," she challenged, "we're talking about my lack of job skills and you've been avoiding telling me about your past for weeks now."

"All right—how about a deal then?" he asked.

"A deal?" she asked. "What are we talking about here?" Cat smiled at him and he chuckled.

"Not that kind of deal, Honey," he said. "How about I agree to tell you about my past?" he asked.

"Deal," she quickly blurted out. He laughed again and pulled her in for a hard, smacking kiss.

"You haven't even heard your part of this yet," he reminded.

"I don't care what it is, I'm in," she agreed.

"Well, I'm glad to hear that, Cat. I'm going to hire you and train you to work as my wingman," he said.

"Wingman?" she squeaked.

"Sure," he said. "Listen, business has been pretty steady and I can use and an extra set of hands. The work is hard and sometimes even physical but I think you'd make a good bounty hunter." Now it was her time to laugh.

"Bounty hunter?" she questioned.

"Yep," he said. "You have good instincts, Cat. And, you've been around the block and know the ins and outs of things."

"Yeah," she said, nodding. "I've been around the block a few times. That doesn't mean I'd make a good bounty hunter, Repo."

"How about you let me be the judge of that, Cat. Listen, we have about two more weeks of waiting for your trial and I can't sit around anymore. I have to work," he said.

"Yeah," she grumbled under her breath, "me too."

"Well, that's where we both agree then. Although I know what you meant—and for the record, Honey, it's not going to happen. Let me train you in what I do and if you like it, great. If not—you don't have to make a career out of it. Plus, it's a way for you to pay me back some like you want." He wasn't playing fair but Cat was quickly learning that was Repo's style. He hit her hard and with everything he had when he wanted his way and she could tell that now was one of those times. He did have a point—she'd be able to start paying him back and it was honest work that would keep her out of trouble—mostly.

"Fine," she agreed. "But it's only for a two-week trial and I can make up my mind from there."

"Sure, Honey," he agreed. "Whatever you say. Now, let's go in and grab a burger—I'm starving."

Cat giggled, "You're always starving, Repo," she teased.

"Well, I'm a growing boy," he said, bobbing his eyebrows at her, causing her to giggle. "Thanks for agreeing to our deal, Cat," he said.

"No problem," she said, jumping down out of his truck. "You can keep up your end of the bargain tonight. I can't wait to hear all about your past, Repo," she taunted. He looked pale as a ghost and she almost felt bad for the guy but she wasn't about to let him off the hook. Cat wanted to know just what she was getting herself into and then, if he played his cards right, she'd give him a preview of her unique job skills, up close and personal.

REPO

He walked into Savage Hell and Cat gently slipped her small hand into his own. He never had her pegged as someone who'd be shy or intimidated by his MC but they were a rowdy bunch. Cillian smiled and waved him over and he wasn't sure how Cat was going to feel about being thrown directly in the lion's den but he was about to find out.

"There aren't many women here," she loudly whispered.

"No," he said. "Tonight's church and women don't come to that. Otherwise, their Ol'ladies would all be here."

"Ol'ladies?" Cat asked.

"Sure," Repo said and shrugged. He forgot that she wasn't from his world. "It's what bikers call their women."

"Oh," she said. He could almost see her wheels turning. She was an open book and right now he knew exactly what she was thinking.

"Yeah," he whispered into her ear. "You'll be my Ol'lady, Cat," he assured her. She smiled up at him and nodded. Cillian stood from his barstool and shook Repo's hand.

"I'm Cillian James," he said to Cat laying his Irish accent on a bit thick. The women that hung around Savage Hell were always trying to cozy up to Cillian but he had a wife and kid at home. Still, it didn't stop his Irish friend from putting on a good show to make the women swoon.

"Cut it the fuck out, man," Repo grumbled. Cillian feigned shock and Repo laughed. "Don't go acting all butt hurt, Kill. You know what you're doing."

"What's he doing?" Cat asked, seeming oblivious to his charms. "I'm Cat by the way," she said, holding out her hand. Kill took her hand into his and smiled down at her.

"Good to meet you, Cat," Cillian said. "Repo has a good eye—you're quite lovely."

"Oh—now I see," Cat said. "You are very charming and Irish to boot. I'm betting all the women around here don't give you much peace." Cillian and Repo both laughed.

"My wife would have my balls if I paid any other woman a bit of attention," Cillian admitted.

"Man, Viv already has your balls. I'm pretty sure she keeps them in her purse or something," Repo teased. "Savage around?" he asked. Repo looked around the bar for their Prez but didn't spot him or Bowie.

"Back office," Cillian said. "With Bowie." He smiled and winked and Repo groaned, rolling his eyes.

He leaned into Cat's body and whispered, "Savage is our

Prez, and his husband, Bowie, and wife, Dallas don't live far from here. Bowie is a club member too."

"Wow," Cat breathed. "He has a husband and a wife? That's hot," she muttered under her breath. Repo threw back his head and laughed at her statement and she shrugged. "Well, it is," she grumbled.

"Well, I just needed to let him know that I'm going to be out of town for a bit still," Repo said to Cillian. "Would you mind telling him? I better grab our dinners and get Cat out of here before church starts," he said. "You know how Savage doesn't like guests hanging out during our meetings."

"Right," Cillian said. "Good thinking. It was lovely meeting you, Cat," he said, giving her his best smile and flirtatious wink.

Cat giggled, "You too, Cillian." Repo took her hand and pulled her along behind him to the front of the bar. He had placed a to-go order earlier and he paid for their food and took the bag.

"Ready?" he asked. He wanted to get Cat out of Savage Hell before she changed her mind about him, about them—about everything he wanted to do with her tonight.

"Cat?" They both turned to find Jackson Hart standing by the front door. Cat smiled but Repo could tell that it wasn't genuine, not reaching her beautiful green eyes.

"Jackson," she said. "It's good to see you."

"You too, Cat. What are you doing here?" he asked. She looked up at Repo and he could see it in her eyes, her silent plea for help.

"We're picking up dinner and then heading out. How do you two know each other?" Repo asked although he was pretty sure he already knew the answer to his question.

"Um," Cat squeaked. "Well, you probably already guessed, Repo," she said.

He looked Hart over and scowled. "Aren't you a cop?" he accused.

"Yeah," Hart said. "Well, detective but close enough. Why?"

Repo barked out his laugh. He felt mean and God help him, he wanted to fucking punch Hart for ever laying a hand on Cat.

"We should just go, Repo," Cat pleaded, tugging at his arm. He handed her their bag of food and she groaned. "Shit," she whispered.

Repo rounded back to face Hart, pointing a finger into the guy's massive chest. "She's off-limits, Hart," Repo growled. "Got it?" Hart smiled and held up his hands as if in surrender.

"Sure, Repo," he agreed. "But Cat and I haven't been together for a long time if it makes you feel any better." It didn't—not one bit. All Repo could think about was his friend putting his hands on Cat and it drove him half crazy.

"Aren't cops supposed to uphold the law?" Repo spat. "Or is hiring a prostitute legal now?" As soon as he said the words, he wished he could take them back. Cat gasped and he was almost afraid to look back over at her. But he was a masochist, so he did and when he realized she was on the verge of tears, her eyes full of unshed sadness, he felt like complete shit.

"It was nice to see you again, Jackson," she almost whispered. She handed Repo the back of food back and opened the front door, walking out into the parking lot. What the fuck had he just done?

"Nice, asshole," Hart said. "I'm not sure what's going on between you and Cat but I'm pretty sure you just blew whatever chance you had with her. God—don't you have one fucking clue how to treat a woman?" He didn't and that was evident every time he opened his mouth and fucked things up with Cat.

"Fuck," Repo spat. He brushed past Hart, not bothering with being polite. No, he didn't have time for that. Cat was hurt and if he had to bet—running scared. The trouble was she had no place to go and he wouldn't be able to find her if she disappeared.

Repo stepped out into the parking lot and quickly looked around. Panic overtook him making him feel more scared and worried than he ever had in his life. His childhood flashed in front of his eyes—being left by everyone he loved and now he'd be able to add Cat to that list. It didn't matter if they hadn't slept together yet, that was just sex. She had snuck under his defenses when he wasn't paying attention and wormed her way into his heart. He had feelings for Cat that he never had for any other woman and that scared the shit out of him. He turned to go to the back of the lot, knowing that if he started driving to look for her, he'd be able to cover more ground. When he got to his pick-up and noticed her shadowed figure sitting in the front of the cab, he felt like he had the wind knocked out of him. The relief of finding her in his truck was almost too much.

He pushed past his fears and anxiety and opened the door to his pickup, climbing into the front seat next to her. He reached over the back and put their food on the back seat. "I fucked up," he whispered.

"Yeah," she spat. "You did."

"You didn't run," he said.

"No," she said, defiantly raising her chin. Cat stared out the front windshield, refusing to even look at him. She had been crying and that made him feel like even more of an ass. "I made you a promise, Repo and I keep my word. Plus, where would I go?" He hated to think that if Cat had another option besides having to be with him—sitting in his truck, she'd take it.

"You know I don't see you that way, right?" he asked.

Cat barked out her laugh but didn't look at him still. "I heard what you said, Repo. It sounded pretty clear to me that you said exactly what you were feeling at the time. You called me a prostitute," she said. A small sob escaped her chest and he pulled her across the seat to sit on his lap, grateful she allowed him to do it.

"I think it might be time for me to keep my word to you now, Honey," he said. "I believe I promised you a story about my past in exchange for you not running." He knew that laying it all out for her would be the only way he'd be able to convince Cat that he didn't mean the ugly words he said back in Savage Hell.

"Yes," she agreed. "That was the deal."

"I was angry and lashed out at you when I realized that you and Hart knew each other. You know—really knew each other?" he asked.

Cat sighed, "If you're trying to say that we had sex, we did. He was one of my regular clients a few years back and then well, he wasn't. Jackson stopped calling and I just figured he moved on. It's an occupational hazard. Guys either find a real girlfriend and don't need to pay me for sex anymore or their wife or girlfriend finds out what he's been doing with me and puts a stop to it. I just figured Jackson fell into one of those categories."

Repo wasn't about to out Hart and tell Cat that he was deep undercover at the time he stopped seeing her. It was something that was still ongoing—his involvement in bringing down the Dragons. They were Savage Hell's rival club and liked to cause trouble at every turn. Things had been pretty quiet lately, with Hart's undercover guy in place as the club's Prez. Still, most of the guys in Savage Hell were just waiting for the other shoe to drop and things to get ugly between the rival clubs again because it was bound to happen. There was just too much bad blood between them.

"I don't want to talk about you having sex with my friend, Cat," Repo insisted.

"Fine, but you knew what I was when you met me, Repo.

You had your chance to let me go but here we are," she said, looking down their entwined bodies as if proving her point.

"Yeah, but you don't know who I am, Cat. I'm worried that once you do, you won't want me anymore," Repo whispered. Cat framed his face with her small hands, rubbing her thumb over his bottom lip, sending little sparks of electricity straight through him.

"I haven't even had you yet, Repo, and I can promise you that I'll still want you once you come clean. Just spill it," she insisted.

"I'm you," he simply said. She looked up at him and blinked.

"Come again," she said. "You're me?"

"Yep," he said. "At least I was you, Cat. When I was a kid, my mother got sick—cancer," he said.

"I'm sorry," she whispered. "That's awful."

"It was," he agreed. "I was scared out of my fucking mind for her and there was nothing I could do to make things better. She died when I was a teenager and my dad—well, let's just say he couldn't handle losing her. He started drinking and then gave up completely and took off. I was alone in the world with no one else to turn to. Child Protective Services started sniffing around and the last thing I wanted was to end up in the system for two years. No one wanted to adopt a sixteen-year-old kid. They want a baby or at least a cute kid who still had potential to become whatever they molded him or her into. So, I took off and I lived on the streets."

"Like me," Cat whispered. Repo stroked his big hand down her back and smiled.

"Just like you, Cat," he agreed. "I had to do whatever I needed to survive. I started selling myself to whoever was paying—women, men, it didn't matter. If they had cash, I did whatever they wanted." Repo remembered that time in his life as hitting rock bottom. He tried not to think of having to meet up with people in seedy motels and dark alleys to pleasure them. Hell, he only let himself think about that time in his life when he was drunk or just plain feeling sorry for himself. That was the past and he didn't like to look backward.

"You turned tricks?" she asked. "But you're so—good," she assessed. He could hear the shock in her voice and he chuckled. She did believe him to be so much better a person than he was.

"You have too much faith in me, Cat," he said. "I did what I needed to do to survive and I'd do it all again too. Maybe that's why I can't fight this connection to you anymore."

"Because you feel a link to the person I am?" she questioned.

He shrugged, "Sure," he agreed. "And, I can see the person you could be. Hell, I was nothing, Cat. I was a stupid kid who took risks and did some dangerous shit. Then, one day I woke up and decided I wanted more for myself. I wouldn't change who I was or what I did to get by. I won't be ashamed of my past but I refuse to let it decide my future."

"Ahh—so, that's where your job offer comes into play,

Repo," she said. "You're trying to give me options to be a better person?" She almost sounded as though she was accusing him of something and his red flags were going up.

"It's not like that, Honey," he said.

"Well, then, how about you tell me what it is, Repo," she spat. Yeah, she was pissed.

"I offered to teach you the ins and outs of being a bail bondsman because I want to keep you close to me, Cat. Hell, I don't care about your fucking past or making you a better person. I just want you to agree to stay with me," he insisted. Cat opened her mouth as if she wanted to protest and he covered it with his hand.

"Before you go and accuse me of wanting to keep you around for the payoff—you're wrong. Maybe that's what this started out being but it's changed, for me at least. Tell me it's changed for you too, Cat," he breathed. He could feel her smile under his big hand and when she nodded, Repo slowly pulled his hand free from her lips.

"It has for me too, Repo," she admitted. "I was just afraid to tell you because I worried that you'd turn me down again."

"I'm done with denying us both, Cat. I want you and I don't give a fuck about the consequences." Repo framed her face with his hands and hesitated just a breath away from her full, pouty lips. He wasn't about to force himself on her but God, he wanted to.

First, he needed to know one thing. "Tell me you're done with that life, Cat," he almost begged. "I won't share you with anyone else, Honey. If you can't make me that promise then this stops here," he said. It sounded like he was giving her an ultimatum or making a threat and maybe he was but the thought of anyone else putting their hands on Cat pissed him off.

Cat didn't seem to flinch at his demands. He worried that she'd hesitate with her answer but when she didn't, he could feel his damn heart beating like it was going to thump right out of his chest.

"I'm done," she whispered against his lips. She pulled her cell phone free from her back pocket and handed it to him. "You'll need to hold onto this then," she said, thrusting the phone at him. He took the phone from her and looked it over.

"You want to give me your phone?" he asked.

"Yeah," she breathed. "I keep getting text messages from clients wanting to know when I'll be back here for a call. If we're going to make this work, you're going to need to hold onto my phone for me."

"Are you afraid that you'll be tempted to take a job?" he asked. If that was the case, this thing between them wouldn't work. He didn't want to have to force her to accept his terms. He needed her to want to give up that life, if not for him then for herself.

"No," she quickly said. "When I say I'm going to do something or in this case, not do something, I stick to my word. But, I need you to believe me. I want your trust, Repo and this is me giving you a symbol of my trust in return." He opened up his glove compartment and shoved her phone in.

"We'll go out tomorrow to get you a new phone," he promised.

"You don't have to do that, Repo. I don't have anyone else I need to stay in contact with besides you and I'm constantly with you." Repo smiled and kissed her. He loved that she didn't want to talk to anyone but him but she was forgetting one major issue.

"You'll need to call and give the courthouse your new number. Otherwise, they won't be able to call you back in. I'll give it to your new lawyer too. He should be able to reach you directly," Repo insisted.

"Thanks," she whispered. "I just wish this whole mess was behind me." He did too. He wanted Cat to be free and clear from her past. Repo just hoped like hell she'd want him to be a part of her future—whatever that looked like.

"It will be soon enough," he said although he had no right to make her such a promise. He had no idea what was going to happen next. All Repo knew was that he wanted her and not taking her was going to prove impossible. He had pushed her away for two weeks now and his cock wasn't willing to wait another minute.

"I need you, Cat," he growled. He helped her straddle his jean-clad erection and when she rubbed her pussy against him, he could feel her heat through her jeans.

"I want you too, Repo," she said. She looked around the parking lot as if she was expecting an audience but the place was pretty dead tonight.

"They're all inside for church," he said. Repo pulled her

down and sealed his mouth over hers loving the way she sighed against his lips. She wrapped her arms around his neck and deepened their kiss.

"You taste so fucking good, Honey," he breathed.

"You too, Repo," she said. He loved the way she seemed a little out of breath from everything he was doing to her. "Help me out of my jeans?" she asked. Repo hesitated. Did he want their first time to be in the cab of his pick-up truck? "Don't overthink this, Repo," she said.

"I just picture our first time to be—well, a little different than you and me fumbling around in my pick-up, Honey," he admitted. "You deserve more than a quick fuck."

She stroked down his cheek with her small hand, cupping his jaw. "That's the sweetest thing anyone has ever said to me," she whispered. "We can take our time when we get back to your apartment, Repo. Please, just fuck me now."

"How can I say no to you when you beg me so pretty, woman?" he teased. He pushed her back against the steering wheel and unzipped her jeans, loving the way she helped him by shimming out of her skintight pants. Repo worked them down to her knees and she leaned forward against his body, giving him better access to finish pulling them free from her legs. He tossed her jeans onto the passenger seat and watched her as she worked her t-shirt over her head, leaving her completely bare.

"Shit," he barked. "You weren't wearing a bra or panties," he said. It sounded like more of an accusation than praise.

Cat giggled, "You don't sound happy about my lack of

undergarments, Repo," she accused. He palmed her breasts in his hands, loving the way she filled them.

"Not unhappy about it," he said. He dipped his head to suck her taut nipple into his mouth and God, she tasted like heaven. Cat ground her wet folds against his body and he needed more. She reached between their bodies and unfastened his jeans, pulling them down just enough to let his cock spring free. Repo hissed out his breath when she ran her hands up and down his shaft freeing a little pre-cum from the tip.

"Fuck, Cat," he whispered. "That feels so good." She smirked up at him and he knew she was going to be trouble from just that one look.

"I wonder if you taste as good as you look, Repo," she sassed. She ran her fingers over the top of his cock to gather the droplets that had escaped his overly anxious dick and raised them to her lips, sucking them clean. God, all he could think about was how fucking sexy Cat would look with her lips wrapped around his throbbing shaft. It was enough to make him just about shoot his load before he even got into her body.

She made a humming sound around her fingers and he couldn't take anymore. "Enough," he growled. He raised her heated core to cover his shaft and thrust into her body, groaning out his pleasure.

"Repo," she whispered. Cat kissed him like a starving woman. She couldn't seem to get enough of him and when she started to move her hips, Repo knew he wasn't going to last long. He grabbed her hips to get some of his much-needed control back and pushed up into her, thrusting as deep as he could go.

"Yes," Cat hissed. "That feels so good, Repo." He loved that she seemed to like it a little rough. Cat threw back her head and rode him like she had lost her ability to control herself, taking every ounce of pleasure he was giving her and giving him so much more in return.

"I'm going to come," she cried out.

"Do it, Honey. I won't last much longer. Come for me," he ordered. Repo watched her ride out her orgasm and he had to admit, she was so fucking sexy it made him lose his damn mind. He followed her over, spilling himself into her hot core, not giving a fuck that he forgot to wear a damn condom. Hell, maybe he wanted to take a chance with Cat and tie her to him somehow.

"Wow," she whispered and collapsed against his body.

"Yeah," he agreed.

"That was the first time I've ever—" she stopped mid-sentence and he wondered what she was going to say next.

"Ever," he prompted.

Cat shyly looked away. "Ever had an orgasm with a man," she whispered.

"Ever?" he questioned.

"Well, I faked it plenty of times. You know, put on a show and promised that it was the best one ever. I've had an orgasm before but usually on my own, with a vibrator. I guess I never wanted to let go with anyone else. Maybe it was a matter of trust," she said.

It made him feel crazy things that Cat was admitting that she trusted him enough to let herself go with him. "Thank you for trusting me, Honey," he whispered against her lips. She sweetly kissed him and smiled.

"Can we go home now? I'm starving," she said. Repo chuckled and lifted her off his lap.

"Put your clothes on and then we can go back to my apartment. Tomorrow, we'll head back to Tennessee." She nodded and started pulling on her clothes.

"Deal," she said.

CAT

They left early the next morning for Tennessee and Cat felt about ready to collapse. Repo didn't give her the chance to sleep very much and she had to admit—being in a man's bed was new and exciting to her. Sure, she had shared a bed with men before but when their time was up, she got dressed, collected her money, and left. She had never spent the entire night with someone before—another first like her orgasm with Repo. Of course, he was thrilled to be two of her firsts and she was wondering if she'd ever end up being any of his firsts.

"We have about another two hours if you want to get some sleep, Baby," he said. Cat was used to him calling her Honey but she had to admit that every time he called her "Baby," her heart felt like it did a little flip flop in her chest.

"What happens when we get back to Tennessee?" she

asked. It had been bothering her all night and into the morning. Would he want to send her back to the bedroom she slept in before their little trip or was he going to allow her in his bed? Would he want that from her? God, she felt so unsure of herself and the whole situation, she worried that she was going to do or say the wrong thing and fuck everything up between them.

"What do you mean?" he asked.

"Well, are you going to want me in your bed, for instance?" she asked.

"Yes," he almost growled.

Cat giggled, "All right then," she teased. I'll unpack my meager belongings into your room.

"Speaking of belongings," he said, not so subtly changing the subject. He seemed just as shy to talk about what was happening between the two of them as she felt. "You're going to need some new things if you're going out on a few jobs with me. I got a call just before we left Huntsville today. I'm thinking about relocating to Gatlinburg," he paused at her gasp. If he moved to Tennessee would that mean that once her court appearance was over, he'd toss her out?

"You're not going back to Huntsville?" she asked. Repo didn't look at her, just stared out the windshield of his truck.

"I'll have to go back to pack up my shit and grab my bike but I'm thinking about starting new. I bought this cabin to use as a home base and the only thing that was keeping me in Huntsville was my club. Savage Hell is a part of a bigger organization called the Royal Bastards and well, I can patch into one of their clubs in Gatlinburg once I get settled." Cat's heart sank at hearing him use the word, "I". She had her answer, he wasn't going to be including her in his move and where did that leave her?

"You mind if I crash at your place until I can afford one of my own?" she asked. Repo finally turned to look at her and she almost wished he hadn't. He looked pissed off enough to tear her apart. "What?" she questioned defensively.

"Don't go and get any crazy ideas that me moving to Tennessee puts an expiration date on us, Baby," he said. "I'm not telling you this because I'm planning on moving you out. I'm trying to fish for a way to get you to agree to move in with me, Cat."

"Wait—you want me to move into your place in Gatlinburg?" she asked.

Repo shrugged like it wasn't a big deal but to her, it was. It was a fucking huge deal. "But we've only known each other for a couple of weeks now, Repo. You can't mean that you want me to permanently move into your place."

"I can and I do," Repo said. "Don't make this into something more than it is, Baby. I want to live in my cabin full time and I'd like for you to be there with me. Hell, if it makes you feel any better, don't use the word permanent. Call what's happening between us a day by day thing," he offered. The problem wasn't the word choice but the fact that he was asking at all. If she was being completely honest with herself, she wanted what he was asking for. Hell, she'd be fine with the whole "permanent" situation if he asked her for that—but he hadn't. He wanted her for now and that would have to be enough for Cat because she wasn't ready to walk away from him, not yet.

"So, how bout it?" Repo asked. "You want to shack up with me?" He sounded like he was teasing but Cat could hear the anticipation in his tone. This was something Repo wanted and that made her a little giddy.

"Well," she taunted. "Let me think about this." She tapped her finger to her chin and couldn't hide her smile. "I mean, I have so many other options for where I could live." Repo reached across the seat and grabbed her thigh, giving it a playful squeeze. "You think this is a good idea?"

"Yeah," he breathed. "But, if this isn't something you want I can help you figure out an alternative." Cat didn't miss the undercurrents of disappointment in his voice.

"No," she quickly said. "I'd like to move into your cabin with you Repo. Your home is beautiful and honestly, I'd love to see where this goes between us—if that's okay with you."

"More than okay," he agreed. "I'd like that, Cat." She smiled and wrapped her hand around his where it still sat on her leg.

"You hear that?" he asked. She listened for a minute and shook her head.

"Hear what?" she questioned.

"It sounds like music coming from my glove compartment," he said. Cat reached forward and pulled it open, recognizing the muffled music from her cell phone's ring tone.

"It's my phone," she whispered as if the person on the other end might be able to hear her. She quickly handed it to Repo as if it offended her in some way. "You answer it," she insisted.

"You sure?" he asked. Cat quickly nodded her agreement.

"Yeah," she said. "I already told you that I don't want that life anymore." She was pretty sure that the unknown number that popped up on the screen was one of her clients. They never used their real cell phones when they called her; most of the time calling her on a burner phone they bought for just such an occasion so that their significant others didn't catch on.

"Hello," Repo answered putting the call on speaker. He looked over at her giving her a flirtatious smile and wink.

"I'm trying to reach Catrina Linz," a distorted voice said. The strange voice almost sounded robotic-like something from a science fiction movie.

"Who the fuck is this?" Repo growled into the phone.

"Someone who's looking for Catrina Linz," the voice said again.

"Well, you can't talk to her until you tell me who this is and what you want with Cat," Repo insisted.

"This is a family matter. I'm a friend of her family's and I called to tell her that her mother is dead," the voice said. It was creepy and sounded devoid of human emotion. Repo cursed into the phone and the person laughed as if they were amused by his outburst.

"Catrina always did keep colorful company," the voice

taunted. "Please relay the message that she needs to contact her family at her earliest convenience." The mysterious person on the other line ended the call and Cat took the phone from Repo and tossed it back into the glove box and quickly snapped it shut.

She looked over at Repo, his scowl firmly in place and she felt about the same way. "You think that they were telling the truth?" she whispered. "Do you think my mother is dead?" Cat wasn't sure how she felt about that. She hadn't seen her mom in over eleven years and it wasn't as if her mother had reached out to her over the years. No one had—not her mom or Liam. As far as she was concerned her life was better for not having a relationship with the woman who called her a liar when Cat told her that her step-father was raping her. How could a mother do that to her child? How could she turn her back on her flesh and blood for a man who didn't deserve to draw his next breath?

Liam on the other hand—him she missed. Her younger brother would be a full-grown adult by now and she often wondered what type of man he had turned into. God willing, Liam had found a way to steer clear of their step-father and make a break from that shitty little town they grew up in.

"I don't know," Repo breathed. "How about you let me reach out to some of my contacts and I'll find out for sure for you. Didn't you say that you didn't leave things on a good note with your family?" he asked. That was an understatement. A relationship between Cat and her family was non-existent.

"Yes," she said. "I haven't spoken to my mom in over eleven years and the same with my brother, Liam. After I left, no one came looking for me so I figured that I was better off without them and vice versa." She realized that her family didn't give a shit about her disappearing from their lives and that hurt like a son-of-a-bitch but she got by just fine without them.

"I'm sorry," Repo said. "That had to hurt—walking away from them and not looking back. A part of you had to want your mom to admit she was wrong and be on your side. I know that's what I would have wanted." He held her hand in his big hand, gently rubbing his thumb over her palm.

"Maybe," she said. "I was just a kid and it hurt like hell that my mother didn't believe me over some man. He took everything from me and no one believed me. No one was on my side." Cat didn't hide the small sob that bubbled up inside of her chest. She liked that she didn't seem to need to hide any part of herself from Repo.

"I'm on your side, Honey," he promised. "You will never have to worry about that." Cat nodded, too emotional to say anything. Repo made her pretty promises but a part of her still wondered how long he would be on her side. The one thing that life had taught her was that promises were usually made to be broken but this time, when Repo broke his word, he'd be effectively breaking her heart too and she wasn't sure she'd be able to handle that.

"What do you want to do about your mom?" he asked. "I mean, we can turn around and head back to—" He stopped talking and Cat looked over at him. "I don't know where you're from, Cat." He grimaced and Cat giggled.

"It's not a big deal, Repo," she assured. "I'm from a little town in Maryland and I don't want to do anything about my mom. She didn't bother to come looking for me so why would I go home to watch them lower her into the ground?" She knew she sounded like a cold-hearted bitch but she honestly didn't care. It was how she felt and nothing would change her mind. Not even getting a call from a stranger, telling her that her mother had passed, would get her to go back home.

"Whatever you say, Honey," Repo agreed. "But, if you change your mind, I'm all for a road trip."

"I appreciate that Repo but I won't change my mind. I learned a long time ago that I need to watch out for myself. Whomever that was on the phone could have been lying. We have no idea who that even was and I'm supposed to run home?"

"My offer stands," Repo said. "How about I have some guys check into whether or not the story is even true and then we can go from there."

"Thanks," Cat said.

"Anytime," Repo said. He smiled over at her and she felt as if her damn heart skipped a beat again. Yeah, that would be something she'd need to get used to.

REPO

Repo moved Cat into his room as soon as they got back to his cabin. There was no way he'd let her even think of staying in his spare bedroom. He knew she was trying to put up a brave front but he could see the nagging concern in her eyes. He had convinced her to bring her cell phone into the cabin to charge in case their mystery caller tried to reach out again. She told him she wanted nothing to do with her old life and that included her cell phone but he convinced her to let him hold on to her cell.

He called his friend Ryder to have him reach out to his military contacts to possibly trace down the number and person who had called. One thing he had learned from his time with his club—they all had special talents that would get him the information that he needed, one way or another. Savage and Bowie also agreed to call in a few favors and do some digging and Repo didn't know if he'd ever be able to repay them. He was going to have to have a conversation with Savage about leaving Savage Hell and finding a new MC in Gatlinburg but that would just have to wait. Right now, his priority was helping Cat get through this tough time and finding her some answers.

He finished cleaning up the dishes from dinner and decided to find Cat. He was trying to give her some space and his cabin was plenty big enough for that. He searched the house over, finally finding her soaking in a tub full of bubbles that made him want to strip bare and join her even though he wasn't much of a bubble bath lover.

"Hey," he breathed, looking her over. "You want company?" Finding her naked and soapy was derailing his plans. He fully intended to ask Cat on a real date—something that neither of them was accustomed to. Hell, he hadn't been on a real date in his entire life and he was betting that the same was true for Cat.

She opened her eyes and smiled up at him, "Sure," she said. Cat watched as he stripped bare and when her eyes rested on his erection he let the little moan he was holding in escape his parted lips.

"Shit Cat," he grumbled. "You keep looking at me like that and I'm going to forget why I came in here." She scooched up in the tub, leaving room for him to climb in behind her. He stepped into the warm bath water and sunk in behind her body, pulling her back against his front.

"Why did you come in here, Repo?" she almost whispered. He wrapped his arms around her body and kissed the top of her head. He knew she was on edge lately and he could feel the anxiety rolling off her body in waves.

"I came looking for you to ask you a question Cat," he said. God, why was it so hard to ask her out? He knew her in the most intimate way a man could know a woman but he was still worried that she'd deny his request.

"Shoot," she ordered.

"I—um, I wanted to ask you if you'd go on a date with me. You know—a real date. We can get dressed up or not—whatever you want. I'd just like to take you out," he said.

Cat turned to straddled his lap and framed his face with her hands letting the soapy water drip down his beard. "You don't have to do that, Repo. I'm not the type of girl you're probably used to—you know the ones who need to be wined and dined?" Repo barked out his laugh. If Cat only knew just how inexperienced he was in all this.

"I'm not sure if you realized this, Cat but I'm just as new to this whole 'dating' thing as you are. If we're laying everything out on the table here, I've never been on a date in my life. I mean, I hook up with women but that usually doesn't last for more than one night and definitely doesn't start with getting dressed up and going out to dinner," he said.

"So, you've never been on a date? Ever?" Cat asked.

"Nope," he said, smiling at her. "Never. I'm guessing you haven't had many dates either, Honey."

Cat shook her head—her wet, blond hair spilling over her shoulder. "No," she said. "I didn't have that type of life—you know, before. I've already told you how things were for me and dating wasn't ever high on my list of priorities. Hell, I barely survived daily life, so dating wasn't even on my radar."

"Then that's an even better reason to say yes to me, Cat," Repo argued. "You have a lot on your plate right now with your court date and your mom. Let me take your mind off all that shit," he offered. He rubbed his erection against her belly and she gasped. He was just as worried about all the shit they had going one because whether or not she knew it, he wanted to be a part of her life—permanently. He was going to ride out the mess with her court date, not because of the money he'd lose if she took off but because he'd miss the hell out of her if she disappeared from her life.

"Say yes," he begged because he wasn't above begging her to get what he wanted. Repo pulled out all the stops, kissing his way down her neck. Her body was still so new to him but he loved how she responded to him every time he touched her. Cat writhed against his body, shamelessly rubbing her wet hot core against his cock.

"Yes," she whispered. "I'd love to go on a date with you, Repo," Cat agreed. He kissed his way down to her soap covered nipples and sucked one and then the other into his mouth. Cat straddled his cock and let him slip inside her body. He loved the way she was so vocal with him, moaning against his neck at the pleasure of having him inside of her.

"You feel so good," he whispered into her ear. "You are so fucking good, Cat," he said.

"You too," she stuttered. "Please just love me, Repo," she

moaned. God, that was the only thing he wanted to do to her. He was already falling for her but there would be no way he'd tell her that. It was too soon for shit like love or feelings getting in the way and messing things up. No, he'd take what he could get from Cat and keep her for as long as humanly possible.

He pumped in and out of her body, sloshing water over the edge of the tub and when she shouted out his name, her core tightening around his cock milking it, it was almost too much. He pumped into her body a few more times, losing his seed deep inside of her just before she collapsed onto his chest.

"Thank you for agreeing to go on a date with me, Baby," he growled.

Cat giggled, "Where are you going to take me?" she asked.

"Well, what's your favorite food?" he questioned. There was so much he didn't know about her. So many things he needed to learn about Cat—his Cat.

"Um—I'm not sure. Usually, I eat whatever is available. I don't get much chance for fancy food choices. Or choices for that matter," she said. It nearly broke his heart hearing that she had to live a life without choices but he also understood her and the decisions she had to make. It made him want to take her to all his favorite places in town and there were many. He'd just have to convince her to go on more than just this one date with him.

"How about I take you to my favorite steak house for

starters and then we can have dessert at a little ice cream place around the corner. How does that sound?" he asked.

She smiled and leaned in to gently kiss his lips, "That sounds perfect," she said. "Thank you, Repo." He swatted her ass, splashing water out of the tub again, causing her to squeal.

"Let's get ready for bed," he ordered. "It's been a long ass day with our drive and I'm tired. Tomorrow, we'll go shopping to pick up some new clothes for you."

"That's not necessary," Cat protested. Repo pulled her against his body for another kiss—this time he wasn't in a hurry to let her go.

He broke their kiss leaving them both breathless. "I know it's not necessary but I want to. Besides, I need a few things myself, if we're going to get dressed up. If you haven't noticed, Honey, I'm not much of a fancy dresser. I'm more of a jeans and t-shirt kind of guy," he admitted.

"Yeah," she said. "But, I kind of like the way you look in your jeans and t's."

"Noted," Repo said. "Now, let's go to bed so we can get an early start tomorrow. We have a full day of shopping and then a date to go on." Repo watched as Cat climbed out of the bathtub and he did the same, grabbing a towel to wrap her in. She wrapped it around her body and walked into the master bedroom, stripping from her towel to slip into his bed. Yeah, he was going to try to keep her for as long as possible, and then he'd fight like hell for more time with her because letting her go wasn't an option for him.

Repo woke early the next morning and stretched. Cat slept curled into his body and when she didn't stir, he decided to let her get some extra sleep while he made a few calls. He was able to put feelers out yesterday when they got to Gatlinburg but it was time to get some answers about her mother. He also had the little matter of coming clean with Savage to handle. He owed his club's Prez that much and so much more. Savage had saved his life more times than he could count and having to admit that he was walking away from Savage Hell, from the men he had come to think of as brothers, felt like he was taking a knife to his chest.

"Yeah," Savage barked into the phone. "This better be good Repo."

"Good to hear your voice too, Savage," Repo said.

"We just fucking talked yesterday. You woke me up and so help me if you wake any of the kids, I will drive to your fucking cabin and beat your ass." Repo chuckled at the "shushing" noises he heard coming from the other and of the call.

"Sorry," Repo lied. "I just needed to check in to see if you and the guys came up with anything on Cat's mom yet?"

Savage sighed into the phone, "Well, the information was true. Her mom did pass a few days ago. I'm sorry, man."

"How did she die?" Repo asked. He knew it would be what Cat wanted to know. She had wondered about it last night over their cozy little dinner for two in bed and he told her he'd try to find out details for her.

"She had been sick for some time and this is the part that sucks." Savage paused and Repo could hear him rustling around on the other end. "Sorry, man," Savage whispered. "I didn't want to wake Bowie and Dallas. I'm in the kitchen now and can talk more."

"Sorry again about calling so early," Repo said.

"Not a big deal," Savage said. "Cat's mom would have been fine if she had gotten medical attention earlier. The medical records that Ryder got a hold of showed that she could have beaten it if she'd gotten help. He said it was some form of cancer but she never got any help. Hell, she probably didn't know she was sick until it was just about too late—poor woman. If Cat wants to go home for the funeral, I'm afraid it's too late. Her mother was cremated without much fanfare or a service of any kind. I'm sorry. That's all I have to report man. You guys good?"

"Yeah, I just have some shit I need to get off my chest," Repo said. He wasn't sure how the hell he was going to tell Savage that he was leaving the club and Huntsville to start over with Cat in Tennessee.

"I get it, man—you like this woman, Repo. She's become important to you and you want answers. I felt the same way about Bowie and Dallas when I first met them. It's hard to put into words how it knocks you on your ass when you find the person, or in my case, people, you are meant to be with. It sure did me." Repo wanted to tell Savage that he was way off base about what he had going on with Cat but he couldn't. He wouldn't outright lie to one of his best friends.

"I promised Cat some answers," he said. God, he sounded like a defensive dick and Savage knew exactly what he was doing. Repo was deflecting, denying, and running from the truth.

"You'll get there, man. I know it's hard to admit when everything's so new but take some advice from someone who knows you better than most people?" he asked.

"No," Repo grumbled. Savage's laugh rang through the phone and Repo held it out and studied it as if it had offended him in some way. "Fine—let's have it then."

"Just give her a chance to get to know you, Repo. You're a good guy—deep down. I mean, really deep, deep down," Savage teased.

"Thanks for that," Repo spat.

"No, in all seriousness, man, I think you deserve some happiness, and what if she can give that to you? What if Cat's the person for you and you're so closed off that you miss your chance. Don't miss your opening, Repo." Savage stopped talking and for just a minute, Repo thought he dropped the call.

"You there, man?" Repo asked.

"Yeah," Savage said. Repo took a deep breath and let it out. It was now or never and if he didn't tell Savage his plans now, he might chicken out altogether.

"I do have one last thing I need to talk to you about," Repo said. He cleared his throat and decided to just barrel through it. "I'm moving to Gatlinburg full time, Savage. I always planned to move here and live in my cabin year-round but never found a good enough excuse to. I have one now—Cat and I could both use a fresh start, man."

"What about the club and your life here in Huntsville?" Savage questioned.

"I love you guys," Repo said. "You're my brothers but I need to do this. It's something I've been wanting to do for a long time. This place feels like home to me. You know my past and where I've come from, man. I've never really had a home and I think it's about damn time I put down some roots."

"With Cat?" Savage questioned.

"Yeah," Repo breathed. "If that's what she chooses. And, I'm going to do everything in my fucking power to help her decide that this is right. We're right together."

"Good for you, man," Savage said. "I'll text you the information for our sister club over there and you can get in touch with Ace. He's the Prez of the Smokey Bandits. They are our sister charter of the Royal Bastards and I'm sure he'll have no problem making the patch transfer. I'll call him this morning to put in a good word."

"Thanks, man—for everything," Repo said.

"No problem, Repo. I'll be in touch as soon as we hear anything else about Cat's mom. Be careful, man, and remember what I said," Savage ordered as if Repo would be able to forget any of his friend's little speech about letting

Cat in. If he was being honest with them both, he already had let her not only into his life but also into his heart.

"Will do, Savage. Thanks," Repo said, ending the call. It was time to wake up his woman and tell her the news about her mom. Then, he hoped like hell she'd still want to spend the day with him and go on their date because it was all he could think about. It was time for him to come clean with Cat about his feelings—all of them and let the chips fall where they may. He was tired of waiting for life to happen for him. It was time for him to take what he wanted and the hell with the rest of it.

CAT

Cat tried on the fifth dress the attendant handed her and honestly, she felt stupid in all of them. This wasn't her—she wasn't a fancy, dress-up kind of girl but she'd do it for Repo. He had done so much for her; this was the least she could do for him.

Repo had woken her just after the sun came up to tell her about her mother's death. Not that it mattered. It didn't change any of her past but a part of her mourned for the woman she used to know. The mother who took care of her when she was a little girl and got sick. Or the mom who taught her how to ride a bike after her father took off. Yeah —that mom was the one she'd remember fondly and miss not the one who all but called her a whore and kicked her out of her childhood house. She'd never honor the woman who let her step-father rape her repeatedly and then accuse her of, "Wanting it".

He told her that her mother's death could have been prevented if she had gotten regular check-ups but Cat knew that there probably wasn't money for things like that. They were dirt poor when she took off and as far as she knew, none of that changed. Her mother would have smiled through the pain, telling everyone she was all right. It was what she did—avoided the truth at all costs, especially when it was ugly. Cancer was an ugly truth and one that Cat was sorry her mother had to endure. The question remained—where her brother was in all of this. If she had to guess, the call they got the day before, was from her step-father trying to trick her into coming back to Maryland. She shuddered at the thought of having to be in the same room with that asshole again. The idea of it made her cringe. She grimaced at her reflection in the mirror and caught Repo out of the corner of her eye as he entered the small fitting room.

"Wow," he breathed. She spun around in the skimpy blue cocktail dress that hugged all her curves and he whistled. "Yeah—we're going to take that one," he ordered.

"You don't think it's too much for our little date?" she asked. His sexy smirk told her his answer before he even said the words.

"Fuck no," he growled. "This is the perfect dress for our date and you're the perfect woman." Cat giggled. He made her feel that way too—perfect even though she was far from it.

"Did you find anything for yourself?" she asked.

"Yep," he boasted. His smile was contagious. "I also called my lawyer friend and he's agreed to take your case. He's going to meet us at the cabin tomorrow morning."

"All right," she agreed. Honestly, with the shit show of her first appearance in court, Cat worried that she was doomed. "Thanks," she said.

"You don't have to thank me, Cat. We're going to get through this together," he promised. He looked her body up and down again and smiled. "The dress is perfect," he breathed, pushing her up against the fitting room wall. The sales lady knocked on the door and asked if Cat wanted to try on a few more dresses and the look on Repo's face was almost comical. Cat covered his mouth with her hand, stifling her giggle.

"I'm good," she said. "I'm pretty sure I'll be taking this dress. Just give me a few minutes to take it off, please."

"Sure thing," the sales lady said. Cat listened for her to leave the posh fitting room and then removed her hand from Repo's lips.

"You're smooth," he whispered.

"You have no idea," she teased. "So, want to help me get out of this dress?"

"Fuck yeah," Repo agreed. He kissed his way down the column of her neck, biting her shoulder when he got down to it. She moaned and wrapped her arms around his neck.

"Zippers in the back," she offered. Repo didn't seem to need to be told twice. He worked the dress open slowly and each inch felt excruciating, having to wait for him to get her naked.

"Change of plans, Baby," he growled. He spun her around so she was facing away from him. "This is going to be hard and fast," he said. "You with me, Cat?" She hummed her agreement and he seemed good with that. "Hands on the fucking wall and spread your legs, Baby."

She loved Repo bossy—it was such a turn on to be told what to do with no room for argument. He hiked her dress up her thighs, exposing her ass to him and when he ran his big hands over her cheeks, she moaned her appreciation. She pushed back against his hands and dipped his fingers through her already wet pussy.

"Repo," she whispered. "Please." She listened as he fumbled with his belt and zipper, dropping his jeans to the floor. Repo filled her and didn't give Cat time to adjust to his demanding cock. He pumped in and out of her body and God, he felt so good. She pushed back against him with every one of his thrusts and before she could stop the moan that escaped her parted lips, it was out and she was sure the salesclerk would be banging on the door, but she didn't. Repo seemed to pick up the pace as if he knew their time in the fitting room was limited. When he snaked his arm around her body and slipped his fingers through her pussy to find her clit, she didn't take long to find her release. He quickly followed her over, spilling into her from behind. Cat felt like she was going to collapse and Repo wrapped his arms around her limp body, breathing into her hair.

As if on cue, the salesclerk rapped on the wooden door startling Cat. "How's it going in there? Can I help you with anything else?" the woman asked. Cat giggled to herself because if the woman could see her at the moment, she'd kick her and Repo out of the store. Repo pulled free from her body and she shouted back something about being right out and the zipper to the dress being stuck. The clerk offered to help her but she quickly assured the woman that she had things under control.

"I'll be right out," Cat shouted. Repo finished unzipping the dress as he righted his clothing and helped her to step free from it. Cat flung it over the door of the dressing room, knowing that the woman was still probably standing there.

"Will you still be taking the dress then?" the woman asked.

"Yep," Cat said. "If you wouldn't mind ringing me up, I'll be right out to pay." She knew that would give Repo a few minutes to sneak out of the dressing room and hopefully not cause a fuss.

"All right," the woman said. "I'll be right out front." Cat listened for the salesclerk to walk away and turned to face Repo, grabbing her t-shirt from him as he held it out to her.

"You think she knows?" Cat asked, tugging the shirt over her head.

"Don't care," Repo admitted.

"Can you sneak out and meet me at the register?" she asked.

"Sure," Repo said. He dipped his head to gently kiss her

lips. "Don't be long," he ordered, handing Cat her jeans. "I can't wait to go on our date." The way he said it made her heart melt a little. She had to admit, she was looking forward to their date too. This was a first for her and she knew it was for Repo. She was excited to see what all the fuss was about, being on a real date.

"Me too, Repo," she whispered. She watched as he disappeared out of the dressing room and Cat set to work finishing putting herself back together. She listened for any signs of them being caught and when a woman's voice accused Repo of being in the ladies' room, she thought for sure they'd be kicked out of the store. She grabbed her bags and headed out of the dressing room to find him.

"I wasn't in the ladies' dressing room," he lied. "I took a wrong turn looking for the men's room." The woman eyed him suspiciously and walked away from him and Repo shot Cat a wolfish grin, causing her to giggle. Yeah, she was looking forward to their date. Cat was sure Repo wouldn't disappoint her in any way.

FOR THE FIRST TIME IN HER LIFE, CAT HAD BUTTERFLIES IN HER tummy. Actual fluttering butterflies and she wasn't sure what to do about them. She was sure that they had everything to do with the sexy biker dressed like a complete gentleman in a suit and tie to boot.

"You look so handsome," she said as she came down the

steps to meet him. His shy smile nearly made her damn heart stutter. Repo usually lived up to his badass persona that when she caught glimpses of his vulnerable underbelly, it made her swoon like a schoolgirl.

Repo took her hand and helped her down the last two steps. She was starting to rethink the high heels he had talked her into. Sure, they were sexy as fuck but she couldn't walk in them to save her life.

"You look hot as hell, Baby," he growled. She stepped into his body and let him wrap her in his arms. God, he even smelled good. "You keep looking at me like that though and we won't leave the damn cabin."

Cat playfully pouted at him and he swatted her ass, "Later," he promised. "Right now, we have dinner reservations. Shit, just saying the word reservation makes me feel like a damn responsible adult." Cat giggled and nodded.

"This whole evening makes me feel like—well, not myself. It's a good thing though. Nice to forget about all the shit going on in my life and just have fun. I've never had that kind of carefree life, you know?"

Repo nodded. He had told her about his life after his mom died and she knew that he hadn't had a carefree life either. But, Repo had made something of himself and she was determined to prove to both herself and him that she could too.

"I get it," he said. "So, how about we go on our carefree, adult date?" he crooked his arm for her to take and she wrapped her arm around his.

Repo was acting the perfect gentleman from the way he helped her into the cab of his pick-up to the way he held her chair out for her at the restaurant. She slipped into the chair and smiled up at him. "Thank you," she said. She looked around the steakhouse he had chosen and suddenly felt very out of place. Cat fidgeted with her napkin and place setting. There were more forks and spoons than she was used to being on one table and she wished she had some idea what each was used for.

"Hey," Repo whispered, taking her shaking hand into his own. "You good?"

Cat quickly nodded, not wanting to let on that she felt so out of place but she was also sure Repo could see through her. "I'm just feeling like I might not belong here," she whispered back.

"Bullshit," he growled. "You belong by my side and that's all there is to it, Honey." He looked up to the waiter who was waiting them out. "We'll take a bottle of your best wine and I'll have whatever is on draft," he said. The waiter nodded and handed them their menus. He went over the specials and disappeared from their table. Cat smoothed her hands down her thighs, worried that her dress was entirely too short. She looked around the crowded restaurant sure that she was garnering unwanted stares from the other patrons who were silently judging her and it was taking all her willpower not to panic and run out of there like a fucking coward.

"You want to leave, Cat—just say the word and we can. But, you are perfect," Repo promised.

"I—I just feel like everyone is watching us," she loudly whispered.

"Can you blame them?" he asked. "We are a good looking couple." Repo puffed out his chest, making her giggle. "There's my girl." Cat could feel her blush at his praise. What was it about this man that made her want to do better—to be better? Hearing him call her, "His girl," made her feel a sense of pride that was just ridiculous but that's what it was. She was proud to be with Repo and tonight just drove that fact home for her.

"Thank you," she said.

"For?" he asked.

"For everything, really. Tonight is perfect and I'm just the luckiest woman in the world that you asked me to be your first date, Repo," she admitted.

He reached for her hand again and she slipped hers across the table to take his. "And, I'm the luckiest fucker in the world that you agreed to let me be your first date, Cat."

REPO

Repo wasn't sure how most first dates usually worked but he felt like the luckiest man on the planet that Cat was his. He couldn't take his eyes off her in that sexy dress and "fuck me" heels. She had asked him to order for her and he decided to go with steak. He knew it was a safe bet since she seemed to love it when he grilled burgers for her.

They talked about everything—their pasts, their futures, and he suddenly felt himself wondering if she saw him as part of her future. He had told her that he wanted to move to Gatlinburg permanently and run his business from his cabin. Hell, he offered her a job by his side, as his apprentice, but he was pretty sure Cat didn't understand the extent that he'd go to keep her close. He wanted her for so much more than a work buddy and it was time that he spelled it out for her and let the chips fall where they may.

Repo helped Cat up into his truck and rounded the front to climb into the driver's seat. He put the keys into the ignition and before he could turn on the truck, she turned to him and smiled, taking his breath away.

"Thank you for tonight," she said. He was being a coward. He made excuses for himself—saying that telling her that he was in love with her in a crowded restaurant wasn't romantic, but he was just being a chicken.

"Cat, I—I think I'm in love with you," he whispered. Repo didn't mean to just blurt it out like that. God, he was fucking this all up but she made him want things he never had before. He refused to look at her, too afraid that he'd see amusement in her beautiful blue eyes and that wasn't something he could stand.

"Repo," she breathed. "Please look at me." He let out the breath he was holding and did as she asked. "I'm in love with you too. I have been since that day in court. I've just been a coward, not wanting to say it in case you don't feel the same way."

"I do," he breathed. "God, Cat—I do." Cat reached across the seat and took his hand into hers.

"Good," she said. "I'm glad I'm not in this by myself, Repo. When you asked me to come work for you, I worried that you were only asking to help me out. Hell, for a while there I thought you were only offering because you felt bad for me. It never crossed my mind that you might be feeling the same way about me. What about all those times you pushed me away? You said you don't fuck with your money," she said.

"I told you that all changed for me, Cat. I thought we already went over all this shit," he growled. "You said you agreed that things had changed for you too."

"They did but you have to understand Repo," she said. "I've never felt like this about anyone else. I didn't believe you at first but these last few days—well, I get it now."

"Thank fuck," he said. "Tell me you'll stay with me, Cat. Tell me that after your court date, you'll come back here and live with me in my cabin." He felt as though he was holding his damn breath waiting for her to give him her answer. "Please, Cat," he begged.

"It's not that easy," she breathed. "What happens if I show back up to court and the judge gives me time? That week you were gone, I did some research and I know what the penalty is in Alabama for prostitution. I'm facing up to a year in prison and a hefty fine."

"I don't give a fuck about the fine," he said. "I'll pay whatever it is, Cat."

"No," she said. "You've done so much already," she said.

"You can work it off," he said. Cat gasped and pulled her hand free from his. "Shit, I didn't mean it like that, Cat. Fuck—I meant that you could work it off as my employee. Shit," he barked. Jesus, he was fucking this all up and when Cat covered her face, sobs racking her petite frame, he groaned.

"Don't cry, Cat," he begged. "I'm sorry—I sometimes don't think before I speak. I fucked up." Cat pulled her hands free from her face and threw her head back and howled with laughter. "What the hell, Cat?" he asked. She couldn't seem to stop laughing. Every time he thought she was finished she'd start all over again.

"Mind sharing what's so funny?" he asked.

"You, this—everything. God, we are quite a pair, aren't we? You are tripping over your words like a teenage boy and I can't figure out when a boy even likes me," Cat said.

"First of all, I'm a man, Honey," he corrected. "Second, I more than like you—I'm in love with you Cat."

"I love you too, Repo," Cat said. He'd never get tired of hearing her say those words to him.

"Then let me help you, Cat. We can figure out the rest later. I don't give a fuck about the money or some damn fine. I think my lawyer we're seeing tomorrow will be able to keep you from serving time," Repo said. His lawyer promised him that he'd be able to keep Cat out of jail but he still had his concerns. If she had to do community service they'd have to stay in Huntsville until her parole was over. As long as they were together, he didn't give a shit where they lived.

"I don't want my problems to become yours, Repo," she said.

"How about if I don't mind, Cat?" he asked. "How about we start calling them our problems and see what happens?" Cat opened her mouth to protest again and Repo covered it with his big hand. "Just give this a chance, Cat." She nodded her agreement and he could feel her smile. Repo pulled his hand free, "Thank you."

"Can we go home now?" she asked. "I'm dying to get out of these shoes." He started his truck and smirked over at her.

"How about you leave the shoes and lose the dress?" he asked. She looked down at her feet and grimaced, making him laugh. "That bad?"

"Yeah," she said. "As long as I don't have to be on my feet, I'll live." Everything Repo had planned for her involved her being on her knees and back, but he'd keep that bit of information to himself.

"Not going to be a problem, Honey," he said.

"Subtle," she teased.

Repo pulled into his garage and shut the door behind him. He was in a hurry to get Cat into his cabin and strip her out of her dress. He was hoping she wasn't wearing any undergarments because that would make his life so much easier. He helped her out of his truck and when her feet hit the floor and she winced, he lifted her into his arms and cradled her against his body.

"Thanks," she breathed, wrapping her arms around his neck.

"No problem, Baby," he said. "I'll have you off your feet in no time," he teased bobbing his eyebrows at her.

He pulled his keys out and unlocked the door and froze when he realized the door was already unlocked. He put Cat down and motioned for her to be quiet. She nodded and pulled off her heels. Repo shoved her behind his body and she took his cue, holding onto his waistband and staying back. His alarm hadn't sounded and he knew that someone had not only broke into his home but disabled his security system. No automatic alarm would be sent to local authorities—they were on their own. He led the way into his kitchen and quietly pulled a corner drawer open, pulling out a Glock he kept in there. He could feel Cat's breath hitch and he wanted to tell her that it was going to be all right but that would alert whoever might still be in his house that they were home.

Repo turned off the gun's safety and grabbed Cat's hand. "Stay with me," he whispered. She nodded and practically pressed her body up against his back. He led them down the corridor that went back to the master bedroom. Whoever broke into their house left the light on in that room, leaving it to shine like a beacon under the door crack for him.

"Is someone in there?" Cat whispered. He looked back over his shoulder and nodded at her. And covered his mouth with his finger, telling her to shut the hell up. She grabbed the back of his trousers and stuck behind him down the length of the hall. He knew that dragging Cat along with him was a fucking awful idea but he had no choice. He wouldn't leave her alone and possibly put her in danger but he also worried that he was walking her right into a trap. How someone had disabled his damn security feed and he hadn't noticed was what pissed him off.

He took a deep breath and pushed the bedroom door

open slowly. He wasn't about to take any chances—not with Cat. Repo pushed his gun into the room, quickly scanning the area and he could tell the exact moment Cat saw the man standing in the corner of the room because it was about the same time he did.

"Who the fuck are you and why are you in my home?" Repo growled. The man smiled but didn't make a move towards them. Repo looked him over and noted that he didn't seem to be armed but he also knew that appearances could be deceiving.

"You always did like the bad boys, didn't you Cat?" the man asked. Cat peeked around Repo's body and he shoved her back behind him.

"You two know each other, Honey?" Repo asked.

Cat peeked out again and shook her head. "No," she said. "I've never seen him in my life." Repo worried that they were dealing with a client who wanted more from Cat and was finding a way to make that happen for himself. He wondered if she had many stalkers in her line of work. One of his former clients had told Repo he loved him after he gave the guy a blow job. That was the last time he met up with that guy. Money or no, he didn't want to take any chances with a client becoming attached to him.

"I'll ask you one more time, man. Who the fuck are you and why are you in my house?" Repo shouted. He trained his gun at the guy's chest. One shot would end him and from the look on the guy's face, he didn't give a shit. His crystal blue eyes showed his amusement and for just a minute,

Repo was sure he knew those eyes. They were Cat's eyes. Shit.

"You're Cat's brother," he guessed.

"Liam?" Cat questioned, stepping from behind him.

"Yeah," Liam whispered. Repo kept his gun pointed at Liam and when Cat made a move towards her brother, he grabbed her arm and pulled her back against his body.

"Let's just figure out why your little brother is here and why he felt the need to break into our home before we get to the hugging and crying part," Repo insisted.

"He wouldn't hurt me—would you Liam?" she asked. Her brother didn't answer her question and when his smile quickly faded Repo worried that Cat wasn't going to like Liam's answer.

"You left us, Cat," he shouted. "How could you just leave me like that? I was just a kid." Repo wrapped a protective arm around her when he felt her body shudder against his. He hated that she was going to have to relive her whole horrible past for her brother.

"I didn't just leave you, Liam. I had no choice. He left me no choice," she cried.

"Who left you no choice, Cat?" Liam asked.

"The man our mother married—our dear step-father," she whispered. "He raped me—repeatedly and when I told mom, she didn't believe me." Liam sat down on the edge of their bed and covered his face with his hands.

"Why would I believe your lies, Cat?" he asked. "Mom told me you were a liar but she never said what you lied about. That's a doozy," he said. "You could have ruined him if anyone believed your story, Cat. Why would you do that to our father?"

Cat gasped, "Our father? You dare call that trash your father, Liam? He's no father of mine. He's a monster."

"No," Liam said, standing again. He took a step towards them and Repo raised his gun.

"Not a step further," Repo warned. "I don't give a fuck who you are, Liam. I'll put a bullet in you if you try to hurt Cat."

"She's using you, man. Can't you see that? My mother told me that's what she does. Cat has always found a way to get just what she needs by taking what she wants from people. She did that to my mother and father and she's using you—Repo was it?" Liam smirked at the two of them as if he knew he was hitting a nerve.

"Shut the fuck up," Repo shouted. "You don't get to talk about Cat that way. Your sister has been through hell and back."

"I see she has you brainwashed too. It's fine really. I didn't come here to convince you that my sister is an awful person. I came here to let you know that mom is dead," he said. "Not that I expect you to care."

"If you don't care about Cat or how she feels about your mother, why are you even here, Liam? Why go to all the trouble to disable my security system and break into my house?" Repo asked. Something just wasn't adding up and seeing how his accusations were hurting Cat was almost too much.

"My mother's last wishes were for me to come here and hand you this," Liam said. He reached into his pocket and Repo panicked.

"What the fuck?" he shouted.

"Don't get yourself all worked up man," Liam said. "I have a letter for Cat in my pocket."

"Pull it out slowly," Repo said. He watched as Liam pulled the letter free from his jacket pocket and held it out towards her. "I've got it, Honey," Repo pushed her back behind his body and took the letter from Liam's extended hand.

"You really need to chill, man," Liam said. "I'd like to head out now, if that works for you, boss man." Repo looked behind himself to where Cat stood. She looked to be completely broken hearted and honestly, he wanted the asshole out of his home.

"Fine," Repo spat. "But you come back here again, I won't hesitate to shoot first and ask questions later."

"Noted," Liam said. He walked past where he and Cat stood, she was still using his body as a shield and a small sob escaped her.

"Stay put," Repo ordered. He followed Liam down the hallway to his front entrance. He didn't trust the guy to let himself out. Cat's brother looked back and flashed him a smile.

"Good luck with her, man," Liam taunted. He seemed like

the type of guy who needed to have the last word and honestly, that was just fine with Repo. He wanted to get back to Cat and make sure she was all right. He shut and locked his front door and pulled out his phone. He needed to rearm his system and then, first thing in the morning, he was going to call a few favors in and get his security system overhauled because there was no way he'd allow a repeat of tonight's shit show—not ever.

CAT

Cat sat on the edge of the bed and wondered what the hell her brother was talking about. From the way he looked at her like he hated her, she knew that her mother and stepfather were feeding him lies. How could her little brother believe them though? They used to be so close when they were just kids. Now, her brother was a stranger to her and there would be no fixing that. She could see that just by looking in his blue eyes. He had already written her off.

"Hey," Repo said. "I did a few quick updates and changed my password. The security system is back up and running. If you'd rather stay at a hotel tonight, I'd understand. I just want you to feel safe, Cat."

"I'll feel safe as long as you're with me, Repo," she said. "Besides, if Liam wanted to hurt me, he would have already tried." She turned the plain white envelope over in her hands, studying it. "I think he just wanted to deliver a message from my mother," she whispered.

"You know, you don't have to open it," he said. Repo crossed the room to sit next to her on the bed. She could tell that he wasn't quite sure what to do about her—as if he touched her, she might break.

"I know that but I'm also curious—it's just my nature," she said.

"It's why I think you'll be great on my security team, Cat. You have natural instincts about people. If it will give you closure, read it. But, I hate seeing you in so much pain, Honey," he whispered. She leaned into his big body and sighed.

"I think I need to do this, Repo," she murmured. "Will you stay with me while I read it?"

"Of course," he assured. Cat pulled the crumpled piece of notebook paper from the crisp white envelope and studied it. It almost looked like someone had crumpled it up a few times to toss in the trash, only to change their mind, fetch it out and refold it. The pencil writing on the paper was faint but she could still make it out to be her mother's handwriting.

Cat cleared her throat, "Cat," she started. "I felt like I couldn't peacefully go on from this world without saying a few words to you. We left so much unsaid and unresolved when you left." Cat almost wanted to laugh at the irony of her mother's words. She hadn't just left on her own. Sure, she wasn't about to stick around and let her step-father continue to sneak into her room and rape her but her mother had kicked her out. She told her that liars and sluts don't get to live under her roof.

"You okay?" Repo asked. She looked down at the letter she was holding and realized that her hands were shaking.

"Yeah," she lied. She felt anything but fine but she needed to get through reading the letter and then, she'd pick herself up, dust herself off and go on—just as she always had.

"While I can never condone the lies that you told about my husband," Cat continued reading. "I can forgive you for them. I wish I had the chance to say these words to your face but you've refused all my requests to return home for one last visit. Liam and your step-father have both told me of your stubborn rejection of my trying to reach out to you. I'm sorry that you are still so hard-hearted but I'm at peace knowing that they and I did everything within our power to reach you. I wish you happiness but more than that, Cat, I hope you get the help you need to get past your lying, scheming ways. Mom." Her voice cracked when she read the last word—no, "Love, Mom" or any kind sediments, just "Mom".

"Fuck," Repo swore.

"It's fine," Cat covered. She was always fine. It was who she was and honestly, she had no idea how to be anything but "fine".

"It's all right to not be, you know?" Repo said. He wrapped an arm around her, finally touching her and she leaned back against him, accepting the comfort he was offering her.

"I know that Repo but you have to remember I've been dealing with this for a long time now. My mother never believed that I was anything more than a scheming little liar. It was too much for her to think that her husband could do what he did. If she admitted that he raped me, she would have had to take some responsibility in all of it. It was probably easier for her to think I was the one at fault than to admit that she brought a man into our house who could do what he did to me. He took everything from me." Cat sobbed and covered her mouth with her hand, not wanting to give in to the sadness and despair that she was feeling.

"It's all right to fall, Cat. I'll be right here to catch you," Repo whispered. He pulled her onto his lap and wrapped his arms completely around her trembling body and for the first time in a damn long time she felt like she had found her home.

Two Weeks Later

Cat had met with her lawyer four times now and her big day in court was tomorrow. This time, Repo had agreed to drive back to Alabama and spend the night at his apartment. Plus, it gave them some time to spend at his club and that was something they both needed—a way to take their minds off her pending court case. Repo's lawyer turned out to be a godsend. He was confident that she'd get off with just a slap on the wrist and maybe a fine but no jail time. That was her hope too but she didn't want to jinx things by admitting it out loud.

She and Repo had spent the better part of the morning packing up his apartment. He planned on turning in his keys after her court appearance and she was just worried that he might be jumping the gun. If she ended up having to do time, would he just go back to Gatlinburg without her? Every time she brought up the possibility of having to go to prison, he'd get pissed off so she decided to keep her questions to herself.

Repo walked into the bedroom holding up her hot pink planner. "Found this on the coffee table," he said, handing it to her. "You want to tell me why you keep a record of all your clients in a hot pink diary?"

"It's not a diary," she insisted. "It's a planner and well, I'm old fashioned. Honestly, I couldn't always afford cell phone service, and this way, I'd have all their contact information in one place. Plus, I could track my appointments and stuff." She flipped through the pages and found the last entry she made. It was from almost eight weeks prior and she realized it was the same day she got arrested and met Repo. That was the last time she had met with a client. It was the day her entire life changed.

"We've known each other for eight weeks now," she said. Outside of her shitty family and her relationship with her best friend, her time with Repo was the longest she had been with anyone.

"It's officially the longest relationship I've ever had," he admitted as if reading her thoughts. "How about you?"

Cat nodded, "Yep," she said. Cat knew that she and Repo had bonded over both being broken and having a shitty childhood and that sucked. But, she was so thankful that she had someone else in her life who didn't judge her because he knew what she had gone through since he had been through the same shit.

He looked at her planner over her shoulder and she didn't feel like she needed to hide all the names of the men she had been with. Faceless, nobodies who meant nothing but a paycheck to her. She'd write just their first name and a contact phone number on the date of their appointment.

Repo pointed to her planner, "What does the 'P' in a circle mean?" he asked.

Cat giggled, "It means that I got my period that date. In my line of work, you can't be too careful. I also was tested every six months to make sure I was clean. It was something that my clients liked—you know, knowing they wouldn't catch anything from me. You were the first man I've ever let take me bareback," she admitted.

Repo smiled, pulling her against his body. "I'll be the last man to take you—ever, if I have anything to say about it, Cat," he growled.

"I think we can arrange that," she promised. "I mean—you did tell me you love me and all," she teased.

"And, you said the same," he reminded. "Unless you've changed your mind," he said.

"Nope," she breathed. Even with all the unknowns in her life, Cat wouldn't change falling in love with Repo. It just felt right being with him—like they fit.

"Good, now let's get some sleep—we have a big day tomorrow," he said. They did and hearing him call her problems his own made her fall in love with him just a little more.

CAT HAD TOSSED AND TURNED ALL NIGHT, NOT ABLE TO REST. Finally, at dawn, she got up and showered, slipping into a pair of jeans and a t-shirt. She needed some fresh air and a walk. What she needed was to figure out what had woken her in the middle of the night from a dead sleep—could she be pregnant? Looking at her planner last night reminded her that she had been with Repo for two months now and in that time, she only had her period once. It started a few days after he bailed her out and drug her to his cabin in Tennessee. She remembered asking him if he could pick her up some tampons and the grimace on his face nearly made her pee her pants laughing at him. That meant that it had been at least seven weeks since the start of her last period and she was always on time. Her monthly cycles ran like trains on a tight schedule. She was about three weeks late and that had never happened to her before. Add in the fact that Repo never wore a condom with her and she was in the eye of a perfect storm. Cat chalked it up to having so much happen to her at once—moving to Tennessee with Repo, her first disastrous court case, their admitting that they were in love with each other and then seeing Liam after all these years—she might have just been stressed but the nagging feeling in the pit of her stomach told her otherwise.

She snuck out of Repo's apartment and put her shoes on in the hallway of his building. She was leaning on the front door to balance herself when she practically fell through, landing up against Repo's massive chest.

"Mind telling me where the hell you think you're going, Cat?" he growled.

She smiled up at him, "Well, good morning to you too," she teased. From the scowl on his handsome face, he wasn't in the mood for teasing.

"I thought you agreed to no more running, Cat?" he asked. She knew that he had trust issues. Hell, they both did but it hurt that he thought she was trying to sneak off and not tell him. Did he believe that she'd go and meet a client after everything they had been through together?

"What do you think I'm doing, Repo?" she hissed. She sounded like she was pissed and well—she was. She didn't like that he could think the worst of her when she had given him no reason to.

"It's not like that, Cat," he countered. He crossed his big arms over his bare chest and she looked him up and down.

"How about you tell me how it is then, Repo?" she said, mimicking his stance.

"You might not think your brother is still a threat but I'm not so sure. Hell, for all we know he was just the first wave and your step-father could be our next unexpected guest. I just don't want you running off without letting me know where you'll be. Hell, I'll go with you but until I know for certain that you're safe, I'll be keeping an eye on you, Cat." She deflated some, dropping her hands at her sides. He wasn't worried that she'd sneak off to meet with another man. Repo was worried about her safety.

"So, you didn't think I was sneaking off to meet a client?" she asked.

Repo looked her over and smiled. "Naw," he said. "I know we haven't been together long but I also know that you wouldn't lie to me, Cat. You've always been honest with me, even when you knew I wasn't going to like what you had to say. I trust you."

She stepped into his body and wrapped her arms around his neck. "Thank you, Repo. Hearing you say those words to me—well, it means everything." She went up on her tiptoes and gently kissed his mouth.

"But, there is something I need to tell you," she admitted. "Something you might not like to hear but it's the truth."

"All right," he said. "Let's have it then."

"Remember our conversation about my planner?" she asked. He quickly nodded and she took a deep breath. It was going to be hard to tell him this next part. She worried that their relationship was too new to face a possible pregnancy scare. She was just going to get it all out—like ripping off a band-aid.

"I always track my periods and the last one came three

days after we met and I think I'm pregnant—well, I'm three weeks late," she breathed. Repo stared blankly down at her and she wondered if he understood anything she had just said. "Repo," she said.

He held up his hand, "Just give me a minute, Honey," he ordered. She watched him as he seemed to work through everything in his head.

"So, you were going to the store to get a pregnancy test?" he asked, finally catching up.

"Yes," she whispered. "I didn't want to worry you unless there was something or in this case, someone to worry about."

"I see," he grumbled.

"I'm not asking you for anything here, Repo. I don't expect you to be happy about this—hell, I don't expect you to be anything at all. If I'm pregnant, I'll figure it all out," she promised. Repo tightened his grip on her arms until it was almost painful.

"Is that what you think of me, Cat?" he asked. "You honestly think I'd walk away from my kid? Does the fact that I told you I'm in love with you mean nothing?"

"You're hurting me," she said. Repo immediately released her arms and took a step back from her.

"I'm sorry," he whispered. "I'd never—" She watched as Repo ran his hands through his unruly hair and she knew that he'd never hurt her.

"I know," she said. "I didn't mean that you wouldn't do the right thing and stand by me, Repo. I just meant that if I am pregnant, it's a game-changer. You didn't sign up for this—any of it. I need to know if I'm going to be a mother before I walk into that courtroom today. I can't focus on anything else right now. Please understand," she begged. Cat reached for him and he shook her off.

"I won't let you push me out, Cat. I know you're scared about today and now this, but I'm going to be there for you and our kid. Give me a minute to grab my shoes and a shirt. I'm going to the pharmacy with you and we'll take this test together. One step at a time," he promised.

"Fine," she agreed. "But I'm pretty sure that I'm the only one who will be peeing on a stick," she grumbled.

REPO

Repo sat on the edge of the tub watching the pregnancy test that sat on the countertop like it had offended him in some way. Cat didn't seem much happier about any of this and in just a little over an hour, he had to have her to the courthouse for the judge to decide their fate. His future with Cat and their possible kid rested in the hands of a person who didn't know her. The judge didn't know Cat's struggles or what her family had put her through. He wouldn't know how she fought like hell to keep a roof over her head and food in her belly. The judge wouldn't understand the choices she made just to survive but Repo did and he was so fucking proud of her even though he had no right to be.

"Marry me," he whispered. He looked up to find Cat

staring down at the test still and he knew she probably hadn't heard his question. "Cat," he said, clearing his throat.

"I heard you, Repo," she said. "I'm just not sure how to answer you. When we started all of this." She paused and pointed between the two of them. "You said that we wouldn't make each other any promises or plan for a future together. We were both too damaged for that and who knows, maybe I still am. But, this is all happening so quickly—I just don't know how to answer you. I won't be your obligation or your burden," she insisted.

"Never," he said. Repo stood from his perch on the side of the tub and wrapped an arm around her. "Never that, Cat. I've been honest with you through all of this. When we started together, I believe that it was just going to be a 'here and now' kind of thing but you quickly became so much more than that to me. I can't explain any of this—our crazy connection or how I feel that I can't live without you even after only spending eight weeks with you. I want you, Cat—all of you. I want to plan a future and a life together no matter what that test tells us. Say you'll marry me, Cat." He sounded like he was begging her to tell him, yes but he didn't give a fuck. He'd get down on his damn knees and beg if that's what it would take for her to agree to be his wife. He never wanted anything more than he wanted her—that part was true.

Cat wiped at the tears that were now streaming down her beautiful face. He stopped one from falling from her soft cheek with his thumb and dipped his head to gently kiss her mouth. "Say yes," he whispered against her trembling lips.

The slight nod of her head gave him so much damn hope but he needed the words from her. "Is that a yes, Honey?" he questioned.

"Yes," she stuttered. "I'll marry you, Repo." He picked her up and spun around his master bathroom, causing her to squeal. "Put me down," she protested. The alarm on his phone went off, indicating that the test should be finished and he stopped spinning around, letting Cat slowly slide down his body.

"Not too late to rescind your proposal," she said. Her frown said it all but there was no way in hell he'd want to take any of it back.

"I wouldn't take back one single minute with you Cat," he admitted. "I've loved every second of being with you—even when you were fighting to get away from me and being a complete pain in my ass—I still loved it. I love you, Cat. That pregnancy test won't change how I feel."

"I guess it's time to face the music," she said, picking up the test. She studied it for a few minutes and then handed it to him. "You read the directions—pregnant or not?" Repo looked down at the white stick with two pink lines and smiled.

"Pregnant," he said. "We're going to have a baby." The old Repo would have laughed his ass off at the fact that he'd gotten her pregnant but then again old Repo didn't ever see himself settling down or having a family—ever. Meeting Cat changed all that for him—she changed him and made him want so much more out of life.

"Shit," she cursed. "What the hell are we going to do, Repo?" she asked.

He kissed her forehead and pulled her against his body. It felt like he was holding his whole world in his arms. "First, we're going down to the courthouse and fighting like hell to keep you out of prison. Then, how about we go to the clerk and get hitched. I know there isn't a waiting period in Alabama. We can just walk in—that is, if you want to."

"I want to," she said. "But what if—" Repo sealed his mouth over hers before she could get the rest of her question out. He knew what she was going to say. Cat was worried that she was going to have to serve time. What she didn't understand was that if she did, he'd be right there waiting for her every step of the way. He packed up his apartment just to show her that he believed in her—he backed her. If he had to unpack his shit and stay right there in Huntsville, waiting for her to get out, he would.

"No what if's," he growled. "Now get dressed—we have a future to get to." Repo let her go and picked up the positive pregnancy test she had dropped onto the sink counter. For the first time in a very long time, he felt like he had a future. Before he had just been living day by day to get by but now—he had something to live for. Or, in this case—two someones.

His lawyer met them in the courtroom and made a show of looking down at his watch. Yeah, he knew they were a little late but he and Cat needed to work through the fact that they were going to be parents.

"Sorry we're late," Cat breathed. She looked up at Repo and smiled. They had agreed to get through the hearing first and then they'd share their news. Besides, he wanted the first people to know about his kid to be his club—his brothers. Savage had texted him earlier that morning to tell him that he had some news about Repo joining their sister club in Tennessee. He promised Savage that he and Cat would stop over just as soon as they were done at court. Then, he could hopefully share all their happy news.

"You're up next," the lawyer promised. "You ready?" Cat nodded. Repo knew that he wanted her to plead not guilty and that he hoped Cat would share some of her story with the court—try to appeal to the judge's soft side if he even had one. But, Repo worried that spilling her guts and her ugly past for a courtroom full of people would be too much for her.

"Catrina Linz," the bailiff called from the front of the courtroom. Repo kissed her cheek and smiled down at her but honestly, he felt just as nervous about all this as she looked.

"You got this, Baby," he promised. Cat nodded and followed her lawyer to the front of the room, standing behind the big desk. The bailiff introduced the court case to the judge and when the judge asked how Cat wanted to plead, he felt like he was holding his damn breath.

"Not guilty, Your Honor. With an explanation," she quickly added. She had a different judge this time. This judge was an older guy, probably in his mid to late fifties and he looked like he'd be stern as hell. Repo would be afraid of the guy if he was in Cat's shoes. The judge looked over his readers at Cat and nodded.

"Let's hear it then," he ordered. The lawyer had gone over the rules of the courtroom, one of them being not to speak unless asked to. She was doing such a good job and Repo was so damn proud of his woman. He could hear her voice shake and knew she was nervous but Cat quickly recounted her ugly past and abusive asshole step-father and every sorted detail she had to spell out for the courtroom made Repo feel sick. He wished he could go to her and comfort her but that wouldn't be allowed. Instead, all he could do was stand by and silently watch as the woman he loved told her hellish story.

When she finished, the courtroom was so completely silent Repo could hear the judge's sigh. "That's quite a story you have there, Miss Linz. I understand what drove you to become a prostitute but it's still a crime and you admitted that you did it—right?" Cat hung her head and gave a little nod. Repo worried that they had gotten a judge who didn't give a fuck about extenuating circumstances and Cat was going to pay the price. Shit.

"You mentioned that you've been working to turn your life around," the judge said. "Want to tell me how?"

"Sure," Cat stuttered. The lawyer had told her to be careful bringing up the fact that she had gotten involved with Repo. The judge might see Cat attaching herself to a man as a way to keep her old lifestyle and break free from having to work the streets. He even used the term, "Kept woman" and Repo wanted to tear him apart.

"I've met someone," Cat admitted. Repo's groan filled the courtroom. She was doing just what the lawyer told her not to. Cat looked over her shoulder to where he sat and smiled at him. "He's the most wonderful man I've ever known. He's taught me to believe in myself and know that I can do better—be better. I'm going to start working for a security company and although I'll be learning the ropes at first, I hope to make it my career. I won't go back to the streets or my old life. I can't," she whispered, cupping her unnoticeable baby bump. "I'm going to be a mother and a wife—that is if I don't have to serve time, I'm getting married right after this." She shrugged as if it wasn't a big deal but Repo knew it was important to Cat. Hell, it was important to them both.

"I want to be the kind of mother mine never was. I'll be there for this baby and my future husband. I want the family I never got but always dreamed of when I was a little girl." The judge dropped the papers he was holding onto his desk and sat back in his chair. He studied Cat over his reading glasses again and Repo knew that she was being weighed and measured. He just hoped like hell the judge could see what he saw in Cat—the caring, kind, loving person she was hiding deep down under her bad girl persona.

"Is this fiancé here today?" the judge asked, looking around the courtroom.

"I am, Your Honor," Repo said, standing from his seat. "I'm the father of her baby and her soon to be husband. I'm also the luckiest fucker in the world." Repo heard the lawyer's moan and Cat's giggle and he couldn't hide his smile. He was never one to mince words and he wouldn't start now.

The judge grunted and nodded. "You seem like a pretty good judge of character," he said. "Do you feel like she's changed since you've met her?"

Repo looked over at Cat and smiled, even giving her a wink to let her know that he had this. "Yes and no," he admitted. Her lawyer groaned again and the judge shushed him. "She's feisty and fiery as hell, just like the day we met. I'm her bail bondsman and well, I didn't trust her to do the right thing and not run. When I found out she had been evicted from her apartment, I decided to take her home with me—worried that I'd lose my money. I fought how I felt about her. We both did actually and I'm pretty sure she all but hated me for the first two weeks we lived together. But then, something changed. She changed. You might not believe that people can do that, especially in your line of work. I'm sure you see people who say that they'll be a different person but then they show up back in your courtroom in just a few months. You have my word that won't be

Cat's story. I was just like Catrina Linz, Your Honor. I was living on the streets and turning tricks to stay alive. You have to do things you'd never dream of doing for food and a dry, safe place to live. I narrowly avoided your courtroom by sheer dumb luck. One day, I decided to turn my life around and make something of myself, so I did. I see that same drive in Cat's eyes and I know she'll be a success story if you just give her the chance to be."

"Thank you," the judge said to Repo. "I'm going to make my ruling now and I've decided to do things a little differently than I normally do. First, Catrina Linz, you will be on probation for the term of one year and you will also pay a one-thousand dollar fine for appearing in my courtroom and taking up my time."

"Yes, Your Honor, thank you," she said.

"I'm not finished," the judge interrupted. "I want you to go to see a therapist as part of your probation. I think it would do you good to work out some of your past issues and help you find a healthy way forward—especially given your circumstances of becoming a mother and wife so quickly after leaving your old life behind." Cat nodded.

"Good," the judge said. "One last thing and this involves your fiancé. If I might be so bold to ask, I'd like to be the one you let marry you today. It will save you time in the Clerk's office and give me great pleasure to see you both find some happiness. I have a feeling that if anyone deserves it, you two do. How about it?" Cat looked back at him and smiled and

Repo knew her answer. He could see it in her beautiful blue eyes.

"Yes," they both said in unison. Repo wasn't sure how but in just a few short minutes he had gotten everything he wanted.

"Perfect," the judge said. "Now, if you'd both approach the bench, we can get you hitched. Council, would you like to stand up for the happy couple? Bailiff, you can be the second witness, if you don't mind." Both men quickly agreed and Repo walked to the front of the courtroom and wrapped his arms around Cat. She was crying and looked so happy but a part of him wondered if she was happy not to be going to prison or happy to be marrying him.

"Good tears?" he asked. She nodded and wiped her nose on the back of her sleeve and Repo was pretty sure it was the cutest damn thing he'd ever seen.

"All I seem to do is cry now," she whispered. "Must be the hormones."

"You sure you want to get married today?" he asked. "If this is all too much, just say the word and we'll wait until you're ready."

Cat suddenly seemed unsure of herself. "Have you changed your mind, Repo?" she asked.

He pushed back a strand of her long blond hair and ran his thumb down her cheek. "Never," he breathed. "I want you Cat—I want you both."

"Then, let's get hitched," she whispered, repeating the judge's words. Repo took her hand into his and stood with her at the front of the courthouse. They stood side by side as they said their vows to love, honor, and cherish each other for the rest of their lives and he could see all the promises she wasn't saying out loud, shining back at him in her beautiful blue eyes. Cat would be his future, his love, and his whole world. She possessed him body, mind, and soul and that was just fine by him.

EPILOGUE

Repo walked into Savage Hell with Cat by his side and he felt like the luckiest fucker on the planet. She had been his wife for all of thirty minutes now and he wanted to tell the whole damn world about their good news—the wedding and the baby. Savage had called him before Cat's court appearance and told him that he had some information about the club he might be able to join in Tennessee. He loved Savage Hell and his brothers in that club. Hell, they had been a part of his life for years now but it was time for him to lay down roots with Cat and their kid at his place in Gatlinburg. If this sister club that Savage knew about let him patch over, he'd at least be able to stay a part of the Royal Bastards.

"Sorry to drag you to my club to start our honeymoon. I promise to make it up to you later," Repo said. He bobbed his eyebrows at her causing her to giggle.

"I'm sure you will," she teased. "And, I don't mind coming here first. I like your club, Repo. It gives me more of a glimpse into your life."

"This is your life too," he said. "Savage Hell is your club now too."

"You sure you want to give this all up?" she asked. "I don't care where we live, Repo."

"I just always thought if I ever put down roots, I'd want it to be at my cabin." He turned to face her and pulled her into his body. Repo needed to remember that things were different now. He was part of a team and Cat had a say in what was next for them as much as he did.

"I love your cabin," she said. "I think it will be nice to start fresh there."

"Really?" he asked. "If you're not sure, just say the word and we can settle anywhere you'd like."

"Really," she agreed. "I think our kid will like growing up there." The thought of filling his cabin with kids and giving them all the love that he and Cat never got as kids, felt right. She smiled up at him and he didn't care that they were surrounded by his club members. Repo pulled her up against his body and kissed her ignoring the catcalls and nasty innuendos.

"You two want to get a room or something?" Savage asked. He slapped Repo on the shoulders and laughed at his joke. Repo found him a lot less funny. What Cat didn't know was that he had booked them a room at a nice little resort on a tropical island and he couldn't wait to whisk her away and have her all to himself for a full week. He was especially looking forward to seeing his new wife in the skimpy bikini he had ordered for her. As soon as she agreed to marry him, he had started setting plans in place to surprise her.

"That's the plan," Repo grumbled. "But, you told me to stop by for news on the new club in Tennessee," he reminded.

Savage nodded, "I hate that you are leaving us, Repo," Savage said. "You will be missed but I've spoken to Ace—the Prez over at Smokey Bandits. They are close to your cabin and also part of the Royal Bastards." Repo nodded already knowing all of that from his research. He had been watching the Bandits and they seemed like a pretty good group of guys. He had spent a few nights at their club and he had to admit, they felt like a good fit.

"Did Ace agree to let me patch over?" Repo questioned

"Well, that's not an easy question to answer," Savage said.

"It's a yes or no answer," Repo said.

"All right," Savage said. "Yeah, he'll let you in the Bandits but not by patching over."

"How the hell does Ace want to play this then?" Repo asked.

"This is the part you aren't going to like," Savage said. "He wants you to prospect for the club."

"Fuck," Repo spat. "I have to start over if I want to be a part of the Bandits?"

"Yeah," Savage shouted over the music. "I'm afraid that might be my fault, man. Ace and I go way back and well, we haven't always seen eye to eye on things. He flat out told me no when I asked him to let you patch over to the Bandits."

"Why the fuck not?" Repo shouted.

"It's a long fucking story and I'll tell it to you someday but let's just say that Ace and I haven't always been the best of friends. I did have fun reminding him that both of our clubs fall under Royal Bastards jurisdiction and he has to take you as a club member one way or the other," Savage said. "Unfortunately for you, Ace chose the hard way and you'll have to prospect."

"Fine," Repo spat. "If that's the way it has to be, I'll do it. I'll have a new life, new wife, and a kid on the way—mine as well go all out." Savage's smile nearly lit up the damn bar once he caught onto what Repo was telling him.

"You guys are going to get hitched?" he asked. Repo nodded and looked down at his beautiful new bride.

"Already done. We got married by the same judge who presided over Cat's case today," Repo said. "Got the wife thing all tied up." He smiled and bobbed his eyebrows at Cat causing her to giggle.

"And a baby?" Savage asked.

"Yep," Cat said palming her unnoticeable belly. "He's already got that worked out too. I'm pregnant."

"Wow man, that's fantastic. You've been busy since you left town," Savage teased.

"Well, I decided that it was about damn time I put down some roots. It's one of the main reasons I wanted to move to my cabin," Repo said.

"I get it, man," Savage said. "You need a fresh start. I'm happy for both of you. We'll be seeing a lot of each other," he promised. "Savage Hell always has business with the Smokey Bandits. I'm sure I'll be stopping by your cabin to check in on you, Repo."

"Any time, Savage," Repo said. "You and your family are welcome at our place anytime." Cat looked up at him and squeezed his hand. "What?" he asked.

"You called it 'our place,'" she said.

"Well, it is now, right?" Repo questioned.

"I guess," Cat said. "I just never had anything real to call my own. Now, I have you and our baby and a home for our little family. Thanks, Repo," she said. Repo dipped down to kiss her and when it lasted a little longer than he planned, Savage groaned.

"Yeah, I'm sticking with what I originally said—you two need to get a room," he teased. Cat giggled and snuggled against his body and Repo was sure that he had finally found his entire world wrapped up in one sexy as hell bad girl package—his Cat, his everything.

The End

I hope you enjoyed Repo and Cat's story. Now, buckle up for your inside sneak peek at Ryder and Tatum's story from book three of the Savage Hell story—Dirty Ryder, coming soon!

RYDER

Ryder pulled up to the red light and balanced his Harley under his big body. It was a perfect day for a ride and when the sexy little brunette pulled up next to him in her little red sports car he was sure his day couldn't get any better. He smiled over to her and nodded. The vixen had the nerve to smile and wink back at him and when the light turned green and she sped off, he knew he had missed his window of opportunity. It was just as well, really. He needed to get home and grab a shower so he could meet with his client who wanted to take a quick flight to Mexico for the night. Honestly, he was looking for a reason to get the hell out of Huntsville for a few nights and he was hoping this trip would turn into something like that. His client told him to clear his schedule for a few days but his business should only take a day. Ryder was hoping that he was wrong and they'd have to end up staying longer in Mexico. It would be nice to kick back and enjoy a few days of downtime and not have to think about anything except his next beer.

The last time he was in Mexico was with his buddy, Whiskey. He had to fly his friend down to that little hell hole his woman was staying in, to get her and his kid. Ryder was happy that his friend had found what he was looking for—a warm, willing woman to go home to every night and the cutest kid Ryder had ever seen. It made him long for things he wasn't sure he'd ever want and that was knocking him off his damn game. Take the brunette in the sports car for example. He would usually have her number and a date set up before the light even had a chance to turn green. Today, he didn't seem to even be able to get out of the fucking gate and Ryder knew that if he didn't do something to get his damn mojo back, he might never find his way again.

He pulled into the parking lot at Savage hell, not sure that he had enough time to check-in and grab a burger but he was starving and fuck it—his client could wait a few minutes. He would just have to eat fast and then get back to his place for a quick shower and grab his gear. Luckily, he kept a "To-go" bag packed for occasions like this.

"Hey man," Savage shouted from his place behind the bar. He was covering for Whiskey while he was taking some much needed time off on his honeymoon. "I didn't think we'd see you tonight. I thought you said you had a client."

"I do," Ryder said. "Or, I think I do at least. I'm heading over to the hanger tonight to meet with the guy and if it works out I'm going to Mexico for a few nights. Sounds like a sure thing though, man," Ryder admitted.

"So, you won't be here for church?" Bowie asked, clapping Ryder's shoulder. Savage's guy was holding their son and Ryder felt a pang of longing for what his friends had built together. They had a family—kids, the big house, white picket fence, and even though the threesome relationship between Savage, Bowie and their woman, Dallas, might not work for everyone, it worked for them. Seeing them all together and happy made Ryder long for something he never really thought about before. Hell, maybe it was because he was getting older or maybe it was the whole ordeal with Whisky and watching his friend finally get everything he wanted out of life. Either way, Ryder was ready for his next step—whatever that might look like.

"Not sure," Ryder said. "Depends on how long this guy needs to be in Mexico. He told me to clear my schedule for the next few nights."

"Understood," Bowie said. "I'm going to take this little guy home and change his diaper. He's ripe." Savage made a face causing Bowie to laugh. "Don't worry, Babe," Bowie said. "I'm not asking you to change him." Savage smiled and nodded. "This time," Bowie quickly added. Savage's smile quickly turned into another grimace causing them both to laugh.

"I'm not sure who's the bigger baby here," Ryder teased. One of his favorite past times was giving his Prez grief.

Savage was always an easy target and had a good sense of humor when it came to making fun of himself.

"Shut the fuck up, Ryder," Savage grumbled. He pointed at Bowie, "I'll see you at home tonight," he promised. Bowie shot Savage a wolfish grin and left through the back of the bar, grabbing the diaper bag on the way out.

"You guys seem so happy," Ryder said. "You are an inspiration," he almost whispered. He looked around the bar as if worried that someone would hear him being so sappy. Hart was sitting in a corner booth talking to a woman; Ryder couldn't see her face though.

"Who's the woman with Hart," Ryder asked. Savage looked over to the corner booth and shrugged.

"Not sure," he admitted. "She's been in here a few times now. She's a looker too." Ryder strained his neck to see if he could catch a glimpse of her face and Savage chuckled. "Geeze man," he said. "Could you be any more obvious?"

"Whatever," Ryder said. "It's been a damn long time since I've had a woman in my bed and let's just say I'm a little on edge." Hell, he was a whole fucking lot on edge but admitting that would make him sound even more pathetic than he was.

"I get it, man," Savage lied.

"Sure," Ryder grumbled. "You have Bowie and Dallas waiting at home for you. How do you get it?"

"Before I found them I was alone and a fucking mess. I didn't let anyone in but when I met them—things just clicked," Savage admitted. He shrugged, "I don't know," he said. "I guess that sounds pretty corny."

REPOssession

"Naw—sounds about right," Ryder said. He ran his hand over his face. It had been a long ass night and he was already hoping that his client didn't want to leave until morning. He needed to get a few hours of shut-eye before flying to Mexico.

"Can I get a burger and fries, man? To go," Ryder said.

"No problem," Savage said. "You want a beer?"

"Better not," Ryder mumbled. "I'll need to keep my head straight in case I have to fly tonight. Thanks though." He looked back over to where Hart sat across from the brunette. Her hair spilled down her back in long curly tresses and all Ryder could think about was grabbing it from behind and yanking it while he rode her ass. Yeah—he needed to get laid sooner than later because lusting after Hart's new woman wasn't going to do anything but land him in deep shit with his friend. And, from the look on Hart's face, he was in deep with the hot brunette and no amount of Ryder's lust-filled fantasies was going to change that fact.

TATUM

Tatum Hart sat across from her older brother, Jackson, listening to him drone on about her life choices and bad decisions but all she heard was, "Blah, blah, I'm not bailing you out again this time, blah." Yeah, she got the message loud and clear. She was going to need to find another place to live because her big brother wasn't about to jump to her rescue again and she really couldn't blame him.

This was the second job she lost in three months and it would also be her third move in less than eight months. She was unstable and unpredictable. Her problem wasn't that she was lazy, as her dear brother liked to put it. No, her issues went deeper than that. She didn't want to take orders from anyone else. Tatum didn't like having a boss telling her what to do, how to do it, and when to show up. And, sure—that put a damper on the whole work thing.

Her past two jobs had been in little clothing boutiques in Huntsville. They were in one of the most prominent shopping centers on Bridge Street and she loved working at both places. Working in clothing retail was her dream. No—scratch that, working in the industry wasn't her dream. She wanted to own a clothing retail store and if she could turn it into a chain, even better. But, that was just a pipe dream since she couldn't seem to hold a job or a place to live.

"What about your roommate?" Jackson asked. "Can't he float you a few months. Hell, he owns the place, right?"

"Sure," Tatum said. "Hugh owns the house and I'm sure he'd be more than willing to let me live there rent-free while I find a new job. It'll just cost me a few blow jobs, is all." She knew she wasn't playing fair. Jackson hated it when she even hinted about having sex which was laughable since she never had—ever. Which was possibly even more pathetic than her current jobless, almost homeless, situation. She was almost twenty-three and had never had sex and yeah—that was more pathetic than losing her job and possibly her home. The truth was, she never found a guy she wanted to give her virginity to. She was an outrageous flirt and loved to tease and lead guys on but that's usually where things stopped. Once a guy realized that she wasn't a sure thing, they took off and left her high and dry.

"Fuck no," Jackson growled. "No fucking way are you giving that asshole, Hugh, a blow job for your room and board. I'm sure you'll figure something out," he insisted.

"Sure, Jackson," she spat, standing from the corner booth

to grab her purse and keys from the tabletop. "I usually figure things out for myself—no sweat. I've gotten pretty good at landing on my feet since Mom died," she said. It had only been six months since her mother passed. Their dad died when she was just eight and her brother was fifteen. It was just her and Jackson and her brother became her stand-in father. Hell, he had bossy and overbearing down pat and she was sure that her father wouldn't have done half the job Jackson had done. He taught her how to drive and even paid for part of her college.

Their mom got sick about two years ago and when she just couldn't function on her own, Tatum moved in with her and took care of their mom. It became who she was and she wouldn't change one thing about spending her mother's last few months with her. It was a gift to have that time with her mom but now she just felt a little lost and so alone.

"Don't go, Sis," Jackson begged. "I'm sorry that I'm being an ass."

"You are being an ass but like I said, I'll land on my feet, I always do." Tatum turned to leave the little bar that housed Jackson's MC and didn't bother to look back to where her brother sat. She'd cave if she did and that was the last thing she wanted to do. Her best bet was to walk out of Savage Hell with her head held high and figure her shit out—to hell with Jackson.

She jumped into her little red sports car that her mother left her and tossed her purse in the passenger seat. It was time for her to go back to her place and face Hugh. She'd probably end up out on the street by nightfall but she'd worry about that later. Right now, she needed to get home and start putting out feelers for her next job.

Tatum turned up her radio, blasting some song that she didn't know the words to but that didn't matter to her. She put the car in reverse and peeled out of her parking spot in the back of the lot, running right into some guy on a bike.

"Fuck," she spat when she heard the grinding of metal. She looked in her rearview just in time to see the biker go down and she wasn't sure what to do next. Tatum put her car in park and cut the engine, jumping out to run around to the back bumper, praying that everything that just happened was just a bad dream. Guys were coming out of the bar to see what all the commotion was about and God, she just wanted to hide under a rock with the way the big, bad bikers were eyeing her. Hart was one of the last guys out and when he saw what had happened, he crossed the lot to confront her.

"What the fuck, Tatum?" he barked. "You okay, Ryder?" he asked the big biker who laid on his side, holding his right leg.

"I think my leg's busted, man," the guy her brother called Ryder said.

"I'm so sorry," she sobbed. "It was all my fault. My music was too loud and I didn't hear or see you and your bike."

"I'll call an ambulance," Savage offered.

"No," Ryder said. "If one of you can right my bike and give me a ride to the hospital, I'm sure I'll be fine. It's probably nothing." Tatum watched as her brother helped his friend off the pavement and when he shouted out a string of curses when he put weight on his leg, she was sure it was broken.

"Here," she said, holding open her passenger door. "Put him in my car since it's close and I'll run him to the hospital." She stood there like a crazy person holding the car door open and her brother just looked her over and scowled.

"You've done enough, haven't you, Sis?" Jackson spat.

"This is your sister?" Ryder asked. Tatum took two steps towards him and awkwardly held out her hand.

"Yeah," she breathed. "I'm Tatum Hart."

"Ryder," he returned and nodded, not taking her hand. "Can't shake now. If I let go of Hart, I'll fall back to the pavement."

"Please let me take you to the hospital to be checked out," she begged. "It's the least I can do."

"You think," Jackson asked. Ryder shot him an easy smile and Tatum realized how good lucking her brother's friend was. She had been to Savage hell a handful of times and had never seen him there. Of course, that might have something to do with the fact that her brother said that every guy in the bar was off-limits. Every time she showed up, he ushered her to the back of the bar as if he wanted to hide her in a deep, dark corner—too ashamed to let anyone see her.

"Go easy on her man," Ryder said. "I'll take your offer, Tatum," he agreed.

"Fine man," Jackson grumbled. He helped Ryder into her passenger seat and was about to shut the door. "Just keep your fucking hands off my sister," he ordered. Ryder gave a mock salute and Jackson slammed the door in his face causing him to chuckle. Yeah, she was pretty sure she liked this Ryder guy. Honestly, she liked anyone who so boldly gave her older brother shit.

She opened her door and nodded to where Jackson watched her. "I like him," she shouted, smiling when her brother's scowl deepened. Yeah, this was going to be fun. But, then again, watching her older brother squirm was always a lot of fun.

Dirty Ryder (Savage Hell MC Book 3) coming soon!

And, before you go...one more sneak peek at a brand new **MC series by K. L. Ramsey. Aces Wild (Smokey Bandits Book 1) will be coming soon. This book will be a spin-off from K.L.'s wildly popular Savage Heat Series.**

ACE

Repo walked into their little club's bar and nodded over at him. Ace had only met the guy a handful of times but he seemed like good people. "You called me in, Ace?" Repo asked. He had and Ace knew that today was going to be tough for the club's new prospect but clubs like the Smokey Bandits didn't need to patch in a bunch of pussies. They needed men who were willing to do the job no matter how dirty or in this case—illegal.

"Yeah," Ace said. "Thanks for coming in so fast, man. I have a little job for you." He knew that as a prospect Repo wouldn't be able to tell him no. Hell, any request, big or small, had to be carried out by the club's prospects or they were out—no questions asked and no second chances given. And, Ace took great pleasure making Repo squirm for his chance to prove himself.

When Savage called him and asked if he'd be willing to patch over one of Savage Hell's members, he refused. Hell, he told Savage to go fuck himself but then his old rival chuckled and reminded him that they were sister clubs under the Royal Bastards and that all he had to do was make a few calls and have the Smokey Bandits put on probation for not following the charter rules they all pledged to live by. So, Ace agreed to Savage's request with a few tweaks of his own. Namely—Repo could join the Bandits, but as a new prospect and work his way up the chains just like everyone else. Savage bulked at the idea but when Repo agreed, the conversation was over. Ace had his new prospect, Repo had a way into the Bandits, and Savage left him the fuck alone.

Repo sat up at the bar and looked across at Ace. He knew better than to talk unless he was told to speak. Repo was following all the fucking rules and damn if that didn't take away some of his fun. "So, you interested?" Ace questioned.

"You and I both know damn good and well that I won't tell you no, Ace. So, what's the gig?" Repo grumbled. Ace chuckled and shook his head at Repo's dramatics. He was right though. Telling Ace no would mean immediate removal from the Bandits.

"This isn't going to be an easy job, man," Ace said. "And, I'm pretty sure that it's not legal either."

Repo groaned, "Fuck, man. Cat will have my balls if I end up in jail. I'm the one who bails people out of jail, not the other way around."

"I get it," Ace lied. He didn't understand the predicament

Repo was in at all. His Ol'lady took off on him to get with another club member and took his daughter with her. It had been months since he heard from Charity or seen his kid and that fucking sucked. He honestly was done with Charity. The minute he let one of his guys touch her, she wasn't a part of his life anymore. But, he wanted to see his daughter. He wanted to be a part of her life but first, he was going to have to find where Charity and that fucker Ratchet took her. As soon as his ex and her new fuck found out that he was on to them, they took off like the cowards they were, taking his little Arabella with them. His daughter was only six months old and the thought of her growing up without him in her life made him sick. She needed him and he needed her—that's where Ace came in.

"You own a security company?" Ace asked.

"Yeah—I manage security for business firms and individual clients alike. I also track people down for their bail bonds." Ace had heard about that last bit from Savage. Repo had gotten his woman out of a sticky situation and he and Cat were now relocating to his cabin in Gatlinburg from Alabama. If he was a betting man and Ace was, he'd bet that Repo had the know-how and skills to bring his baby home to him. Then, Charity and Ratchet could decide to live or die—it was their call. He didn't give a fuck either way. If they wanted to live, they'd walk away and leave him and Arabella the fuck alone. If not, Ace had no problem with killing them both for what they had done to him. Ratchet was one of his oldest friends and taking his woman broke one of their codes. Hell, as far as Ace was concerned, it was the worst betrayal.

"I need you to track down my Ol'lady and daughter," Ace ordered. Repo winced and Ace immediately knew he had heard the rumors that flew around the club about what had happened. Ace heard them too but he didn't give a fuck what the other club members had to say about what went down between Charity, Ratchet, and him. That was no one else's fucking business.

"How long they been gone?" Repo asked.

"A few months now. They took off when they realized I was on to them. Listen Repo," Ace said. He rounded the bar to stand directly in front of his prospect. "As your Prez, I have the right to ask you to do whatever the hell I want. But, this goes deeper than doing me a favor. I'll pay whatever your normal fees are—I just want my daughter back." He knew he sounded like a fucking pussy, all but begging the new guy to help him out but, if that's what it took, he'd do it. Ace wasn't above a little groveling especially if it meant he'd get his daughter back. He wanted her to grow up knowing him. He didn't know his old man and that led him down many wrong, dark paths. He wanted to give Arabella everything he never had and so much more and Repo was his only chance.

"Will you do it, Repo?" he asked. Yeah—he was asking and not telling. Ace meant what he said—he wouldn't use his power as the Bandit's club Prez to get Repo to agree to work for him.

Repo nodded, "Yeah," he breathed. "But, I'm going to need a lot more information. Cat can work this one with me. She's getting quite good at tracking people down who don't want to be found. If they're hiding, we'll find them," Repo promised.

"Thanks, man," Ace almost whispered. He held out his hand and Repo took it, giving it a shake. "For everything."

TRINITY

Trinity walked into the little bar and worried that she was biting off more than she could chew. But, she had a message to deliver, and then she'd high tail her ass back out of there and get back to the right side of the tracks. She set the car seat on the closest table and shook her achy arm. The kid weighed a ton and she was sick and tired of lugging her around. Her sister had left her kid at her house and took off with some guy who looked like he just got out of prison. It was just like Charity to pick the seediest, dirties, bad assed man to make wrong decisions with. It was who her older sister was and Trinity was always there to pick up the pieces when the shit hit the fan. She'd count Charity dropping off a baby at her place as the shit hitting the fan.

Charity was drunk out of her mind and Trinity wouldn't put it past her sister to be high too. Her drug of choice used to be cocaine but Trinity hadn't seen her sister in almost five years. Hell, she barely knew the woman Charity had become, and with the way she just dumped off her kid without so much as a glance back, she didn't want to.

All her sister said was, "I need you to take her to her father. It's the only way he'll leave us alone." Trinity wasn't quite sure what her sister's cryptic message even meant until she walked into the bar and quickly looked around. Every guy in the run-down bar was scoping her out and she suddenly worried that she was making a huge mistake. If one of the tattooed, bearded, bike riding jack asses looking her over was her niece's father, maybe she was better off without him.

"Can I help you?" a tall man asked. She strained her neck to look up at him and noticed that his smile was mean but it didn't touch his eyes. She quickly unzipped the baby's car carrier, revealing the sleeping infant inside. "I'm looking for this kid's father."

"Shit," the man grumbled. She watched as he unbuckled Arabella from her car seat and pulled her free, not caring that it had taken her the better part of an hour to get her to sleep. "She's mine," he admitted. The biker wrapped his tattooed arms around the sleeping baby and cradled her to his body.

"Who the fuck are you?" he rudely asked. "And, why the fuck do you have my kid." Yeah, her sister wasn't ever big on dating guys with manners. Trinity wondered if Charity had made the choices she did to purely piss their father off or if she was happy with them. She was pretty sure her sister's piss poor excuses for boyfriends had everything to do with their father. She and her sister had taken very different paths in life. Her sister looked for every excuse to blame their father for all her failures and Trinity looked past their shitty childhood and made something of herself. She went to college, earned her degree, and worked for a fortune five hundred company and was being fast-tracked for a seat as a vice president. She and Charity were like night and day and there would be no changing that.

"I'm Trinity—Charity's younger sister. I take it you're Ace?" she asked. It was just about all her sister gave her to go on. Charity handed her the car seat with the screeching kid in it, her diaper bag, told her the kid's name and the father's name. That was about it and then Charity was gone.

"My sister dropped off Bella today and asked me to deliver her to you. She said something about you not coming after her if she gave you what you wanted. I'm assuming that's her?" she asked nodding to the baby who had once again settled and fell back to sleep in her father's arms.

"Damn straight. I've had men out looking for her," he looked down at his daughter and smiled. "Her name is Arabella," he corrected.

"Sorry?" she asked, trying to keep up with the change of topic.

"You called her Bella and that's not her name," he said.

"Yeah, well—I'm the kid's aunt and I'd say that earns me the right to call her all kinds of cute little nicknames." Trinity reached out and rubbed Arabella's fuzzy little head. She had to admit—the kid was pretty damn cute but the last thing she needed was to get involved in her niece's life. That would be a giant fucking mistake.

"I take it you and your sister aren't close?" he asked.

His comment felt like a physical assault more than just a comment. "Why would you assume that?" Trinity spat.

Ace chuckled, "Because Charity was my Ol'lady for almost five years and she never mentioned you." *Figured.* Her sister wouldn't have mentioned Trinity's existence because that would have meant that she gave a fuck about her sister. Charity didn't care about anyone else but herself. That fact was evident when she so easily walked away from her kid.

"Right," she said, clearing her throat. "Well, it seems you have it all worked out then and she seems to be in good hands." She again nodded to her sleeping niece and smiled. Were all babies that peaceful when they slept? "I'll just be on my way then," she said. Trinity picked up her purse from the table and pulled the diaper bag free from her shoulder, handing it over to Ace. He took it and slipped it up his shoulder

"Thanks," he said. "For everything. You have no idea what having her back here with me means. I owe you, Trinity."

She nodded, "No need to pay me back, Ace she said. Listen, I know my sister can be hard to live with and I have no idea what happened between the two of you but I know Charity usually means well. I'm sure she returned Bella here for good reason and if that's the case, you must be a pretty decent guy."

"I appreciate that, Trinity," Ace said.

"She just ate an hour ago and my phone number is in the diaper bag—just in case you need me, Ace. I'd love updates about her." Trinity barked out her laugh and it sounded mean. "Up until yesterday, I had no idea my niece even existed. The little bug grows on you I guess. Take care of her." She turned to leave the seedy, little bar because standing in that place for even one more minute would have her changing her mind about leaving Arabella. But, what choice did she have? Trinity had a life to get back to and with any luck, a deal to close. Her company was depending on her and she'd never let them down yet.

ACES WILD (SMOKEY BANDITS BOOK 1) COMING SOON!

1

ABOUT K.L. RAMSEY

*Romance Rebel fighting for
Happily Ever After!*

K. L. Ramsey currently resides in West Virginia (Go Mountaineers!). In her spare time, she likes to read romance novels, go to WVU football games and attend book club (aka-drink wine) with girlfriends.

K. L. enjoys writing Contemporary Romance, Erotic Romance, and Sexy Ménage! She loves to write strong, capable women and bossy, hot as hell alphas, who fall ass over tea kettle for them. And of course, her stories always have a happy ending.

K. L. RAMSEY'S SOCIAL MEDIA

Ramsey's Rebels - K.L. Ramsey's Readers Group
https://www.facebook.com/groups/ramseysrebels/

KL Ramsey & BE Kelly's ARC Team
https://www.facebook.com/groups/klramseyandbekellyarcteam

KL Ramsey & BE Kelly's Street Team
https://www.facebook.com/groups/klramseyandbekellystreetteam/

KL Ramsey and BE Kelly's Newsletter
https://mailchi.mp/4e73ed1b04b9/authorklramsey/

facebook.com/kl.ramsey.58
instagram.com/itsprivate2
bookbub.com/profile/k-l-ramsey
twitter.com/KLRamsey5

BE KELLY'S SOCIAL MEDIA

BE Kelly's Reader's group
https://www.facebook.com/
groups/kellsangelsreadersgroup/

facebook.com/be.kelly.564
instagram.com/bekellyparanormalromanceauthor
twitter.com/BEKelly9
bookbub.com/profile/be-kelly

MORE WORKS BY K. L. RAMSEY

The Relinquished Series Boxed Set (Coming soon)

Love Times Infinity

Love's Patient Journey

Love's Design

Love's Promise

Harvest Ridge Series Box Set

Worth the Wait

The Christmas Wedding

Line of Fire

Torn Devotion

Fighting for Justice

Last First Kiss Series Box Set (Coming soon)

Theirs to Keep

Theirs to Love

Theirs to Have

Theirs to Take

Second Chance Summer Series

True North

The Wrong Mister Right

Ties That Bind Series

Saving Valentine

Blurred Lines

Dirty Little Secrets

Taken Series

Double Bossed

Double Crossed

Owned

His Secret Submissive

His Reluctant Submissive

His Cougar Submissive

Alphas in Uniform

Hellfire

Royal Bastards MC

Savage Heat

Whiskey Tango (Coming soon)

Savage Hell MC Series

Roadkill

REPOssession (coming soon)

WORKS BY BE KELLY (K.L.'S ALTER EGO…)

Reckoning MC Seer Series

Reaper

Tank

Raven

Perdition MC Shifter Series

Ringer

Rios

Trace (Coming soon)

Printed in Great Britain
by Amazon